Best wishes,
Eleanor Rosellini

A Mystery in Maine

Eleanor Rosellini

Illustrations by Elizabeth Vogt

ISBN 0-7414-5023-2

Published by:

INFINITY
PUBLISHING.COM

1094 New DeHaven Street, Suite 100
West Conshohocken, PA 19428-2713
Info@buybooksontheweb.com
www.buybooksontheweb.com
Toll-free (877) BUY BOOK
Local Phone (610) 941-9999
Fax (610) 941-9959

Printed in the United States of America

Printed on Recycled Paper

Published October 2008

Dedicated to the memory keepers of Maine, who enrich the present by preserving the past.

With special appreciation for
Burnt Island Living Lighthouse, Boothbay Harbor
Holt House, Blue Hill
Chase Emerson Memorial Library, Deer Isle

Other Hidden Treasure Mysteries

The Puzzle in the Portrait
The Mystery of the Ancient Coins
The Mystery on Observatory Hill

A Vacation Turns Mysterious

Elizabeth Pollack, ace detective, woke up on a summer morning in Maine and discovered . . . the world had disappeared. She hopped out of bed and squinted through the window. Never in her life had she seen such a fog. It pressed against the glass, thick and ghostly pale. The beach, the islands, the open sea – everything was lost in a dreary mist.

The moan of a fog horn drew Elizabeth closer to the window. Maybe today would be –

"GRASSHOPPER PECAN PIE!"

Kid brother alert! Elizabeth jumped back into bed and pulled the covers over her chin. She squeezed her eyes shut as she heard footsteps clatter up the spiral staircase. She didn't have to look to know who was hovering over her bed. Jonathan would be there, grinning over a fat book in his hands. It wasn't fair, thought Elizabeth. No eleven-year-old girl should have a kid brother whose best friend is *The Encyclopedia of the Totally Disgusting*. In the three endless days of their drive to Maine, he had worked his way up to the letter *R – Revolting Recipes*.

"Add one cup chopped grasshopper to three cups roasted pecans."

Keep your eyes shut, Elizabeth told herself. Breathe deep and slow. He might go away if he thinks he can't annoy you. But it was hard pretending to sleep. She knew her brother was staring at her face, probably only inches away.

"Hey, Elizabeth. I know about the Baker Street Girls."

"What?" Elizabeth shot up in bed. "You're not supposed to be snooping around in my room!"

"I wasn't snooping. I saw a note right there on your night table. And it says Baker Street Girls." He picked up a small piece of white paper.

Elizabeth grabbed it out of his hands and put on her glasses. "It's supposed to be a surprise."

"Okay." Jonathan looked at his book. "Pour nuts and grasshopper pieces into a piecrust and add . . ."

"But I'll let you look now." Elizabeth leaned over and shut Jonathan's book. "I found the note yesterday when I was in town with Dad. It was on the sidewalk right in front of the library. I guess someone dropped it."

She handed the paper back to Jonathan. Scrawled across the top in bold red ink were the words *Baker Street Girls*, underlined twice. Jonathan read the note out loud. "*Chinese scroll -- stolen 1890. Never found. THE MYSTERY MAN. WHO IS THE MYSTERY MAN?*"

He looked up. "Wait a minute! Baker Street. That's where Sherlock Holmes lived."

"I know," said Elizabeth. "So there must be some kids in town who call themselves the Baker Street Girls. I think they're detectives. And they're looking for a stolen scroll. You know, some kind of paper that's rolled up."

"Maybe," said Jonathan. He put down the note. "But I bet they're just pretending. Like we used to do."

"I'm not sure," said Elizabeth, "but I don't think it's pretend."

"Yeah? How do you know?"

Elizabeth didn't answer. Jonathan would think she was weird. But hadn't he noticed how something had changed in their lives? How mysteries just seemed to *come* to them, like metal to a magnet. The village of Stone Harbor was just a speck on the curlicue coast of Maine, but even sleepy little towns have their secrets. She looked down at the words streaming across the crumpled paper. *WHO IS THE MYSTERY MAN?*

"I'm gonna go eat breakfast," said Jonathan. "It smells like . . ." He closed his eyes and sniffed deeply. "Mealy bug

2

fritters with maple syrup." His voice trailed off as he hurried down the stairs. "I want to be finished before Peter gets here."

"Oh . . . right. Peter." Elizabeth took a long, deep breath. Peter Hoffmann was exactly her age, but he certainly wasn't like any other eleven-year-old she knew. She and Jonathan had met him in Germany, while working on one of their most exciting mysteries. She wondered if the State of Maine would be ready for their German friend. A restless mind. A detective kit the size of a small suitcase. And nonstop ideas that could lead to triumph . . . or trouble. Peter would love to have a mystery ready and waiting. All they needed to do was find out if it was real or just pretend.

When Elizabeth shuffled down the spiral staircase, she found Jonathan in the living room eating breakfast with their parents. Usually the wall of windows made the room seem as big as the sky. But now, with a dull curtain of fog, the house felt lonely and small.

"French Toes." Jonathan dangled a strip of French toast in the air before stuffing it into his mouth. Elizabeth ignored him.

"I hope Peter's family doesn't have trouble finding us in all this fog." Mrs. Pollack stood in front of the window warming her hands on a cup of coffee. "That would be something. They come all the way from Germany and have trouble going the last few miles."

Mr. Pollack peered out the window. "Oh, I think they'll be all right. This looks to me like an ocean fog. It's likely the roads are clear inland." He turned around. "By the way, I assume you know what causes fog." Elizabeth nodded her head vigorously. Both her parents were teachers, and the price of not knowing something was a long lecture.

"Well, anyway," said Mrs. Pollack, "if I know Peter, he'll talk the fog into disappearing." Elizabeth saw her mother's lips tighten. It wasn't that Mrs. Pollack disliked Peter. She had come up with the idea herself. They would rent a house in Maine, and Peter would stay with them while his parents took a special tour of New England for librarians. But now that the moment was near, Elizabeth could read her mother's mind. Fourteen days of Peter – the thought was a little scary, somewhere between going to the dentist and being out in a hailstorm.

"Don't worry, Mom. I'm sure Peter's different now. He's probably more, uh, more . . ."

"Mature," said Mr. Pollack.

"Exactly." Elizabeth poured a lazy drizzle of syrup over her French toast and took her first bite.

"Hey, Elizabeth, in Venezuela some people eat hot sauce made with termites." Jonathan had finished his breakfast and was settled on the couch with THE BOOK. "You put chili peppers in the sauce to make it hot, and termites to make it crunchy. But you have to use a special kind of termite."

Elizabeth slapped down her fork. "Mom, make him stop!"

"Jonathan, we've discussed this before. No Encyclopedia of the Totally Disgusting while someone's eating."

"But it's true." Jonathan looked to his father for help.

"Well, not everything that's true has to be discussed at the breakfast table," said Mr. Pollack. He walked over to the couch. "And I wouldn't want to take that book away from you."

"Okay, okay." Jonathan smiled sweetly. "Don't worry, Elizabeth. I'll explain later. And I'll show you a picture too. It's a close-up."

Elizabeth looked over at her brother after she finished her breakfast. She would rather go swimming in a shark tank than be cooped up all morning with Jonathan and his *Encyclopedia of the Totally Disgusting*. Glancing out the window, she could see the world coming back into focus. Far

4

below, a rocky shore and smooth gray sea emerged from the mist.

"Come on, Jon. It's too boring to sit around and wait for Peter. Anyway, he won't be here for awhile." Jonathan didn't respond. He was still cooing over his book. "The fog is lifting, Jon. We can walk down the beach and go to the library in town."

Jonathan jumped up. "Yeah, they might have volume two of my encyclopedia!"

A few minutes later Elizabeth and Jonathan set out. The front yard sloped down to a thick hedge of roses marking the edge of a cliff. Elizabeth stepped through an opening in the bushes and followed a set of rickety wooden steps down to the beach. Leaping over a tangle of seaweed, she landed on a shelf of rock jutting out toward the sea. The water was quiet, as flat and gentle as a pond.

Slowly, they made their way toward the town. Even at low tide, the beach offered no comfortable stretches of flat sand. It was a rocky, come-and-take-a-look beach, full of giant hump-backed boulders and busy little pools left behind by the tide. As they rounded the point, they could see the village of Stone Harbor.

"Oh, I say! This is a nice bit of fog!"

Elizabeth froze. Strange. The voice almost sounded like . . . Sherlock Holmes.

She whirled around and found herself face to face with Peter. He seemed taller than last year, but she recognized the summer pink of his pale skin and the spikes of blond hair pointing up to the sky.

Peter stood with his hands on his hips. "I say! What ho, old chaps!"

"Huh?" Jonathan and Elizabeth spoke at the same time.

"What ho!" He greeted each of them with a cheerful clap on the back.

Jonathan raised one hand. "Oh . . . uh . . . what ho."

Elizabeth automatically turned to German. "*Hallo, Peter! Wie geht's Dir?*[1]"

Peter raised his hands. "No German, please. I am speaking now the perfect English." Elizabeth smiled. Peter was his old self – here less than a minute and already bragging. The three hoisted themselves onto the broad back of a boulder. They sat cross-legged on the flat stone. Peter was full of news. After flying in from Germany, he and his parents had spent a week in New York City. At the hotel, he spotted a suspicious figure and followed his every move. Like most of his cases, this one ended with a stern lecture from his parents. For one thing, Peter had spilled half a bottle of fingerprint powder on the lobby carpet, and then the suspicious figure turned out to be the hotel detective.

"But I am the cat with the nine lives," said Peter. "Everything becomes good. The detective has a policeman brother, and they take me to visit the crime lab." He gave a dreamy sigh. "High tech."

"I know, I know," said Elizabeth. "Technology is the future of crime detection."

By the time Peter's tale was finished, Elizabeth decided not to say anything about the note she had found. Somehow, the Baker Street Girls didn't seem so exciting after all.

Jonathan had been staring at Peter. "Where did you learn your English? You know, that *old chap* stuff."

"I study English in school for three years," announced Peter. "But I tell you my secret to perfectness. Old movies from England. Where they are speaking the *real* English. I watch them and I memorize. Tut, tut, pip, pip, and all that." He stood up. "And I learn songs. Many songs. Now you will see."

Facing out to the open sea, Peter lifted his chin and flung out a tune. Something about hearty lads and blushing

---

[1] *Wie geht's Dir?* (Vee gates deer?) How are you?

maidens. When he started warbling about the gentle orb of love hanging lonely in the sky, Jonathan bent over and held his stomach. "Make him stop. I'm gonna be sick."

Elizabeth shrugged. Peter never did anything halfway. He could probably keep singing until the stars came out. "That's good, Peter. It's really . . . very . . . English. So, why don't you come with us to the library? They let visitors check out books."

"Right ho. Jolly good." Peter jumped down from the rock and waited for the other two to follow. "I say, what's that?" He pointed up towards the bluff, where a large white building loomed over the sea. Thin fingers of fog lingered around the edges.

"That's some old inn," said Elizabeth. "I think it's been closed for a long time." For a moment, she stayed on, gazing up. She usually loved old places in Maine – prim white houses that promised trunks in the attic and secret hiding places. But the empty inn was different, with bare windows staring out to sea like eyes that never closed. She turned away and hurried down the beach to catch up with the boys.

After reaching the harbor, they climbed a steep, sandy path to the village. The main street of Stone Harbor had already come to life. The small grocery store bustled with customers. A few tourists drifted into the town's only gift shop. Elizabeth pointed to a tiny gray cottage tucked away at the end of the street. "That's the library."

"I'll race you there!" shouted Jonathan. Peter and Elizabeth took off after him. By the time they saw the man coming out the library door, it was too late to avoid a collision. A moment later they untangled themselves from a portly middle-aged man with a fierce black mustache.

Peter began fussing over the man, dusting him off and arranging his clothing. "Oh, I say. Frightfully sorry, old boy." Jonathan and Elizabeth gathered up the books scattered on the ground.

Without a word, the man grabbed his books and stomped away. A woman walked at his side, clutching her purse as if they were about to steal it.

"Now if I were you, I'd stay away from Mr. and Mrs. Edmond." An elderly woman, lean and wiry, stood behind them. "They've been summerin' here for years," she continued. "Far as I know, they don't fancy youngsters. But don't let it make you feel bad. Mr. Edmond doesn't seem to fancy much of anyone."

"He's not such a jolly chap, I think," said Peter. "Oh, well . . . tally-ho!" He stepped onto the library's tiny front porch and held open the door for the others.

Elizabeth forgot about the Edmonds as soon as she walked in. She loved all libraries, but this one was her favorite. The two small rooms were as snug as a fairy-tale cottage, with a cozy fireplace and arched windows that looked out to the sea. They walked past the librarian, who smiled at them from behind a wooden desk. Elizabeth led the way to the back room, lined with heavy bookcases.

The elderly woman they had met outside came in with them. She leaned up close to a bookshelf, squinting at the titles, with her rough gray hair almost touching the books. Elizabeth looked at the lady's rolled up blue jeans and wondered if she had been digging for clams.

Suddenly the front door clattered open. Out of the corner of her eye, Elizabeth could see a pink pantsuit and a rounded puff of snow-white hair. A heavy-set woman stood in the doorway for a moment, leaning on a gold-tipped cane. Her large hands sparkled with rings. "Hattie!" she cried as she hurried into the back room. "The letter! It's gone! I think someone took it!" She made her way between the bookcases and lowered her voice as she spoke to the other lady.

As Jonathan and Elizabeth stared, Peter sprang into action. He strode up to the two women. "My dear ladies," he said. "Please allow my help. My business card." He pulled out a white card from his pocket. "I am Peter Hoffmann, detective extraordinaire, from Hamburg, Germany." He swept his hand in the direction of Jonathan and Elizabeth. "And these are my . . ."

"Partners," said Elizabeth, stepping up quickly.

The woman in pink stared at the business card. "*The Three-Star Detective Agency.* Well, imagine that! A group of detectives showing up at a time like this." She motioned for the three to come closer. "I'll tell you one thing," she whispered. "Something strange is happening around here. Something very strange."

A Strange Tale

Peter directed the ladies into two tall armchairs by the back window. "You have much luck today. You have help from the Three-Star Detective Agency. Already we have solved together a mystery. The Mystery on Observatory Hill." In his fast but not-quite-perfect English, he launched into a story about the double mystery they had solved in Germany. Elizabeth was ready to jump in at the first sign of bragging, but Peter didn't take all the credit for himself.

The ladies listened, with a few giggles and some wide-eyed *Oh, my*'s. When Peter was done, they huddled together and whispered for a moment.

"This isn't a good place to talk," said the lady in pink. "Come to our house for tea this afternoon. Three o'clock. We live in Rosewood Cottage, right across from the library. And bring your parents too. We'll tell you all about . . . ," she glanced over her shoulder and lowered her voice, "things that have disappeared."

The whispered words sent a shiver dancing up Elizabeth's arms. Day one with Peter and already a new mystery. "We'll be there!" she said. Elizabeth stayed with the ladies for a few more minutes, then saw Peter motioning for her to leave.

She shook her head. "I'm not through talking. And I still want to get a book."

But Jonathan and Peter had already turned and headed for the door. The librarian stepped out from behind a bookshelf and stared at them as they left.

"Hey, wait!" Elizabeth caught up with the boys at the top of the path that wound down to the beach.

"I *say*! This is a bit of all right." Peter opened his arms to the breeze, gazing at the sparkle of ocean below. The sun had melted away the last bit of fog, cheering up the sea and sky to a lively blue. Even the faded fishing boats in the harbor looked crisp and new.

"I see a seal!" shouted Jonathan. He pointed out beyond the harbor. A tiny head, sleek and dark, bobbed for a moment, then disappeared.

"Jolly good," said Peter. "This is a sign we have luck."

After a scramble across the beach, Elizabeth spotted their rented vacation house perched up on the bluff. The front was a curved wall of windows, giving the house the look of a giant fish bowl. Elizabeth could see her loft room sitting on top like a hat. Jonathan led by a nose as they raced up the wooden steps and dashed into the house. They found the grown-ups laughing and chatting in the living room.

"A case!" Jonathan shouted. "We've got a case! There was this lady in the library. Pretty old. And she was looking at books. Then another lady came in. All fancy with puffy hair and jewelry and a cane with gold on it. And there's a letter and it's gone. Maybe stolen. So Peter gave them his business card, and they want us to . . ."

Mrs. Pollack got up from the table. "Jonathan, hold on! I don't understand a word you're saying. And you haven't even said hello to Peter's parents."

Jonathan and Elizabeth walked over to Herr and Frau Hoffmann[2]. They each gave a shy handshake and a polite *"Guten Tag."* Peter's parents hugged them both. *"Hallo, Detektive."*

Peter stepped in. "English!" he commanded. "In America we speak English. We all agreed."

"Okay," said Peter's father. "I torture you with my bad English." Peter's mother laughed. "And I also."

---

[2] "Herr and Frau Hoffmann" means *Mr. and Mrs. Hoffmann. Guten Tag* (GOO-ten tahg) is German for *Good Day.*

She turned to Jonathan and Elizabeth. "So you find Peter and find a mystery too?"

"We met two ladies at the library," explained Elizabeth. "They live in a little house right on the main street. Anyway, they didn't want to say much right there, but something mysterious is going on in town. They invited us to tea, and they're going to tell us all about it. And the grown-ups are invited too."

"But I don't understand," said Mrs. Pollack. "Who are these ladies?"

"I can't remember their names," said Elizabeth. "But I talked to them for awhile . . ." She glanced at the boys. "Until *somebody* made me leave. They grew up here in town, and they're pretty old, probably about eighty. One of them looks . . . well, kind of like Huckleberry Finn. She told me she used to work at the post office. And the other one, the one who dresses fancy, she moved to Boston when she got married. Then a little while ago their husbands both died, so now the two of them live together."

"I have told them we are perfect detectives," said Peter. "And we solve their mystery."

"That's fine, Peter," said Mr. Pollack. "But we do have other plans for the afternoon. Your parents want to see the model ships at the maritime museum. It won't be open tomorrow, and then they'll be leaving."

"How about this?" said Mrs. Pollack. "I'll take Hans and Helga to the museum. The rest of you can go to the ladies' house for tea. I have a feeling you kids won't rest easy until you find out what this is all about."

Just before three o'clock, Mr. Pollack and the three detectives followed a narrow walking path into town. Peter took the lead, striding along importantly with his oversized detective kit. Elizabeth carried her red spiral notebook and lucky green pen.

At the edge of town, the path met the main road. Just ahead stood the empty inn they had seen from the beach. A hopeful *For Sale* sign stood in the front yard, but not even a perfect summer day could take away the gloom of broken shutters and peeling paint. Elizabeth couldn't imagine anyone being tempted to buy the place, especially with the words painted over the door. *Jeremiah Coffin Inn. 1783.*

As the group reached the center of town Elizabeth ran ahead to a small wooden house across from the library. It was a simple white box of a house, crowded up against the sidewalk. Next to the door, a pink rosebush shot up from a patch of dirt.

"This must be it," she said. "Rosewood Cottage." Elizabeth stood straight, pushing up her glasses and rearranging her ponytail. After the first knock, the door swung open. From somewhere in back came the yipping bark of a small dog.

Elizabeth knew they were in the right place. The elderly lady dressed in blue jeans stood in the doorway. Her steel gray hair, chopped off just below her ears, was straight as rain. Mr. Pollack stepped forward and introduced himself.

The woman motioned them in. "Pleased to meet you," she said. "Hattie Pruitt is my name." She gave Mr. Pollack a brisk handshake. "And I've already met the three detectives." Elizabeth repeated the name to herself so she wouldn't forget. *Hattie.* It sounded hard and definite, like a bang on the table. A good fit.

"And I'm Edna Mancini." The lady with the puffy white hair came up from behind, walking slowly with her cane. Her words floated out softly. "You just call us Hattie and Edna," she added. "Everybody does."

Inside the house a sweet aroma hinted of something just out of the oven. The group followed the ladies into a tidy front room. It had the creaky-comfortable feel of a very old house, with a floor that tilted and windows with thick, wavy glass. On the faded Oriental rug, a round wooden table was set with white cups and saucers.

As the others sat down at the table, Elizabeth wandered around the room. Dainty African violets. Family photos. A knitting bag. And . . . a warrior? She stared at a large statue standing in the corner. The wooden warrior wore a fearsome mask and not much else. She saw Jonathan gazing at the other side of the room. Over the fireplace hung a sword that looked big enough to slay a dragon.

Hattie smiled. "Some of my great-grandfather's treasures," she explained. "He was a sea captain. Sailed all over the world."

Jonathan turned his attention to a plateful of blueberry muffins. Edna and Hattie passed around cups of hot chocolate and tea.

"Now then," said Hattie. "My mother always said you don't talk business until you set down and get to know each other. The children told us some about their cases."

"Very impressive," added Edna. She paused and let Hattie continue.

"Now, Edna and I are detectives too. At least we used to be. See, the two of us, we've been chums since, oh . . . seems like forever. We grew up next door to each other. Had a detective club when we were girls."

"And we worked on real cases," said Edna. "Of course, we did get into a mite of trouble."

"Like what?" Jonathan's eyes brightened.

"Oh, now let's see. There was that fuss about the hair oil. Tell them about the time we smeared up the school house, Hattie."

"Well, see, we were investigatin' some break-ins at our schoolhouse," began Hattie. "We took my Papa's jar of hair grease and oiled that school up good. Door knobs. Windows. Anywhere where you could break in. We figured the thief would reek to high heaven of hair oil, and we'd sniff him out. Trouble was, we forgot to put the jar back. Papa got up the next morning, half asleep. Grabbed the jar of skunk oil for grandma's rheumatism and smeared it all over his hair. Oh, did we catch it for that! Course the break-ins stopped, so we considered it a grand success."

Jonathan nodded his approval as he stuffed a piece of muffin into his mouth.

Edna looked at Mr. Pollack. "But don't worry, we've calmed down considerably since then."

Peter put down his cup of tea. "I say, my good ladies, these . . . how do you call them . . . muffins are jolly good. May I take another?"

"Go right ahead, young man," said Hattie. "You just tear into those muffins. Edna baked them special for today."

As Peter raised himself up to reach across the table, a door banged open at the back of the house. Toenails clicked down the hallway. The furry gray face of a tiny schnauzer appeared in the doorway. As soon as it set eyes on Peter, the dog rushed over and nipped the back of his shorts. Peter straightened up with a cry of surprise. The schnauzer hung on, dangling in the air like a dog in a circus act.

"I say, old chap," said Jonathan. "You seem to have a dog hanging from the seat of your pants."

Edna leaned over and unclamped the dog. "I'm so sorry. Are you all right, Peter?"

Peter waved his hand as he sat down. "It's quite all right. The dog bites only my pants, not my . . . uh . . . not my backseat."

"Now, Daisy. You're being naughty again," said Edna gently. "You know that's no way to treat guests." She turned to Peter. "It's your shorts, I'm afraid. For some odd reason, she's always had a strong dislike of plaid clothing."

"Quite all right," said Peter. He looked down at his red plaid shorts. "I know about dogs. I read many books. We must be friends. Right-ho, Daisy, old girl." Setting his plate

15

on his lap, he pinched off a crumb of muffin and held it out to the dog. Cautiously, Daisy stretched her nose toward the treat. Suddenly she set her front paws on Peter's knees. Before anyone could stop her, the dog snatched the entire muffin off his plate. She disappeared under the table with her treasure. Peter looked down at his empty plate, then popped the crumb into his mouth. "By Jove, I think she likes me!"

While Edna gave the dog another mild scolding, Hattie laughed so hard her eyes teared up. Finally, she pulled a handkerchief out of her pocket and blew her nose. "Well, we've had our fun. Now it's high time we get down to business." She took one more sip of tea. "You see, Edna and I have stumbled onto a mystery."

Elizabeth suddenly remembered the note she had found. "Wait a minute! You must be . . . You must be the Baker Street Girls!"

"And you're trying to find a Chinese scroll that was stolen a long time ago," added Jonathan. "And you're looking for a mystery man."

"Well, I never!" exclaimed Hattie. "You're right, that's for sure. The Baker Street Girls. That's what we used to call ourselves. But I don't think even Sherlock Holmes could have figured that out."

Elizabeth reached into her pocket and pulled out a piece of paper. "It's not really that hard. I found this note on the sidewalk yesterday."

"Why, that's my reminder note," said Edna. Her gold bracelets jangled as she took the note from Elizabeth. "It must have fallen out of my pocket." She waited while Elizabeth opened her notebook. "I'll fill you in on the details," said Edna. "It's going to be a lot to write down. You see, the story of the Chinese scroll started more than 150 years ago. Way back in 1850, a sea captain gave a gift to the town of Stone Harbor. It was a painting done on silk. An ancient Chinese scroll, hundreds of years old and very

16

valuable. The captain had brought it back from one of his trips to China." She set down her teacup. "In 1890, the scroll suddenly disappeared. Stolen! Right out of the display case in the town hall. The crime was never solved, and the scroll was never seen again." Edna stopped talking and looked at Hattie.

"That's when the rumor started," said Hattie. "You see, Edna's grandmother always admired that scroll. She even tried to buy it from the town. When the scroll disappeared, people started saying she was the one who took it."

"And worst of all, the rumors never stopped." Edna's hands fluttered in her lap. "People used to say the scroll was buried with my grandmother. Hidden in her coffin. Years ago there was even some foolish talk about . . . about digging up the grave. It's a disgrace, I tell you. My grandmother was a good, honest woman. Not a thief."

Hattie patted her friend on the shoulder. "All right, dear. Now don't start gettin' all exercised. We know your grandmother didn't take that scroll. And we're going to prove it." She turned to the others. "You see, Edna and I discovered that someone else confessed to the crime. A man."

Jonathan inched up in his chair. "But I don't get it. How do you know? It all happened so long ago."

Edna leaned forward. "It started two days ago. Something very interesting came in the mail. From a friend of Hattie's. You tell them, Hattie."

"Well, you see, my friend lives down in Portland, Maine. Now, Hazel – that's her name – is what I call a keeper. Oh, it pains her to throw things away, especially old things. She's always snooping around in old papers, trying to find something interesting. I don't think anyone in the city of Portland throws anything away without showing it to Hazel."

Elizabeth looked up from her notebook. "Memory keepers. That's what my mom calls people who save little bits of the past."

"Then Hazel's a memory keeper, all right," said Hattie. "She always sends me anything that has to do with Stone Harbor. Well, the other day she sends me an old letter she found. Not a whole letter, just one page. It was with a mess of papers stuck away in the basement of a hospital. I could tell it was written a long time ago. You know – brownish ink and swirly handwriting. Edna's eyes are better than mine, so I gave it to her to read."

Edna continued. "The letter was written by a nurse who was taking care of a man with a terrible fever. The man must have thought he was going to die, because he started . . . saying things. Like he was confessing to a crime. The nurse wrote down his words, exactly as he said them. He said . . ."

Before she could finish, Hattie rose up and stood in front of the fireplace. She spoke in a slow, deep voice. "*I'm the one who took it, but no one knows. The scroll is safe. Hidden away. Hidden away and rolled up tight.*" She looked at the others, her small gray eyes hard and bright. "*The scroll.* Don't you see? He must have meant he took the Chinese scroll. The letter was dated September, 1890, just a few months after the theft. And the man with the fever must have lived around here. The nurse wrote that he kept mumbling something about Stone Harbor."

Elizabeth scribbled down the information as fast as she could. "Wait a minute! The man who confessed. Is he the mystery man? Like you said in your note?"

"Exactly," said Hattie. "My friend only found that one page of the letter. Most of the hospital records from 1890 were ruined in a flood a long time ago. So we don't know which nurse wrote the letter, and we don't know who the sick man was. That's why we call him the mystery man."

Mr. Pollack's eyebrows rose up then took a dive. Elizabeth sighed. She knew what was coming. Something logical and not very encouraging. "I don't doubt what you're saying," he said, "but I have to look at things . . . scientifically. The man with the fever was talking about a scroll, but you can't say for sure he was talking about the Chinese scroll that was stolen. And you can't depend on what people say in a fever. He was probably delirious."

"You're right," said Edna. "It's not scientific. But sometimes . . . sometimes you just *know* things. I know my grandmother didn't steal the scroll. And I know that this mystery man did."

"And here's how we're going to prove it," said Hattie. "First of all, we need to find out who the mystery man was. That might give us the clues we need to *find* the Chinese scroll. If that letter leads us to the scroll, it means the man with fever was the thief for sure."

Peter had been quiet, listening while he guarded his muffin from Daisy. "Excellent case, my good ladies. But I am not understanding one thing. When you came in the library this morning, you said a letter was gone."

"That's right," said Edna. "The letter we told you about – the one that talked about the words of the mystery man – we had it for one day, then suddenly it disappeared. I'm convinced the letter was stolen." She lowered her voice. "I don't know who it is, but someone wants to stop Hattie and me from working on this mystery."

A Theft in the Night?

Hattie sat down again. "Now, Edna. We can't prove someone is tryin' to stop us. The house was locked up good and tight last night. And you know we're always losing things." She poured another round of hot chocolate and tea. "You see, Edna and I, well, we're different in a lot of ways. Now me, I'm as calm as a clock. Except when I get mad, of course. But Edna here, she lets her imagination run wild. Maybe it was all those years living in a big city. You don't trust folks as much as you used to, Edna."

Edna gave a sniff and arranged her gold necklaces. She pointed to a table by the window. "I tell you, Hattie, I saw the letter right there last night." She turned to the others. "Hattie's nephew Tom had us over to dinner. Tom and his son Lenny drove us home."

"Lenny just got his driver's license," said Hattie. "Drives real good, too."

"They waited until we got into the house," continued Edna. "Then they drove away. Let's see. I came in here and waved out the window to Mildred Patterson, the librarian. She was out for a walk. And I saw the letter. It was on the table, plain as day. But this morning it was gone." She paused. "And there was a book with it, a library book, and that's missing too. You see, I wanted more information about the scroll. I found an old book at the library. *The History of Stone Harbor*. It discusses the theft."

Elizabeth continued to write in her notebook. "So the letter is gone, and the history book that talks about the theft is gone too."

"Did anyone know you had the letter?" asked Mr. Pollack.

"Oh, you can't keep secrets in a little town like this," sighed Edna. "We told our families. And I did tell the librarian. And come to think of it, we may have been talking about it at the little grocery store down the street yesterday."

With a sudden frown, Hattie squinted toward the window. "And of course, there are the *summer complaints*. That's what we call the summer tourists. Not the nice ones like you, but the annoying ones." She raised her voice as she walked toward the window. "The ones who poke around and stare in people's houses. Who knows what they might hear?" Elizabeth could see what had set Hattie off. An enormous mustache hovered above the window box geraniums. It was Mr. Edmond, the man they had collided with at the library. He stood on the sidewalk, peering in curiously.

"We're still alive, Mr. Edmond. This isn't a museum yet." Hattie closed the window with a bang. "The summer complaints may be nosy," she continued, "but I still don't hold to the notion of someone stealing that letter and book. I tell you, Edna. You're going to find them somewhere and feel foolish. Anyway, we can get ourselves another copy of that history book. The library in Spencer isn't too far away. I'll ring them up. See if they have a copy of *The History of Stone Harbor*." She walked into the hallway and dialed the telephone.

Edna waited until Hattie was out of earshot. "I should tell you something else. Hattie forgot to lock the door last night," she whispered. "She's getting a little forgetful. I checked the door before I went to bed. I would say it was unlocked for half an hour or so. And come to think of it, I did hear Daisy bark. She's such a yippy little thing, I didn't pay any attention."

Hattie walked into the room a few minutes later. "Now that *is* strange," she muttered. "The Spencer Library has two copies of *The History of Stone Harbor*. They can't find either

21

one. The books aren't checked out. They were either put on the wrong shelf, or . . . someone stole them."

Before anyone could speak, a snap rang out like the crack of a whip. Peter had opened the clasps of his detective kit. He was fully equipped – everything from a magnifying glass to fingerprint powder. Carrying a small bag and a brush, he walked over to the table where Edna had left the letter. "Fingerprint powder," he said. "May I?"

Peter applied a dusting of powder, then shook his head.

"I'm afraid I wiped off the table this afternoon when I cleaned up," said Edna. "I forgot about fingerprints. I guess my detective skills need freshening up."

"Quite all right," said Peter with a wave of his hand. "Quite all right. I can investigate many ways." He took out an enormous magnifying glass and began crawling on the floor. A sudden growl made him spring to his feet and press himself against the wall. It was Daisy, with muffin crumbs still dangling from her long whiskers. Peter slid along the wall and sat down quickly, placing a napkin over his plaid shorts.

Elizabeth laughed. "Well, I guess we've taken the case," she said. "I hope I have all the clues." She looked down at her scribbled notes. "Let's see. The Chinese scroll was stolen in 1890 and never seen again. Then a few months later some mystery man with a fever was in a hospital in Portland, Maine. He started mumbling about a scroll, and the nurse wrote down what he said. *I'm the one who took it, but no one knows. The scroll is safe. Hidden away. Hidden away and rolled up tight.*"

Hattie nodded. "And there was something else. The man kept calling someone's name. It was . . ." Hattie tapped the side of her head as if she were trying to knock a memory loose. "Rebecca! That's it. The mystery man was calling out for someone named Rebecca."

Elizabeth added one more note. *Find out who Rebecca was.*

Jonathan slid out of his chair and began edging his way toward the sword. Mr. Pollack looked at his watch. "Well, I'd say you kids have a lot to think about. But right now it's about time we get back."

"How's this for a plan?" asked Hattie. "The Baker Street Girls and the Three-Star Detectives will think up some ideas and meet here tomorrow morning. Ten o'clock. And I think we can promise you something special to eat."

"We'll be here," said Jonathan. "No problem."

The group got up to leave. Elizabeth turned as they headed out the door. "One more thing. Didn't you say the mystery man talked about Stone Harbor?"

"That's right, he did," said Hattie. "Oh, blast. I wish we still had that letter. He kept muttering something in his fever. Something about looking out to sea, out past the harbor. But at a certain time."

"Don't worry," said Edna. "We'll think of it. We just have to brush the cobwebs out of our brains."

Two hours later, after a short, cold swim, Elizabeth hurried up the spiral staircase to her room. Her father called this room the eagle's nest – a small loft snuggled under the steep roof. Outside, a cool evening breeze skimmed across the water. But here the warmth of the sunny afternoon remained, like a treasure held in a cupped hand.

Elizabeth wrapped herself in a thick sweatshirt. This must be the most beautiful place in the world, she thought. The window at the foot of her bed framed the ocean like a painting. The blue water stretched out so far, Elizabeth imagined she could see the curve of the earth. And now a mystery had come their way. A treasure hunt for a Chinese scroll.

Even the Three-Star Detective Agency seemed better. Peter was kind of weird with all that *jolly old chap* business, but he didn't seem as bossy as he did in Germany. And maybe there was even hope for Jonathan. He must be getting . . .

"And now, for your listening pleasure . . ." Jonathan's head popped up at the top of the spiral staircase. "I shall eructate."

"What?" Elizabeth narrowed her eyes. Every time her brother used a two-dollar word it came straight from *The Encyclopedia of the Totally Disgusting.*

"*Eructate.* It means burp." He bowed. "I proudly present . . . the burping alphabet!"

By the time Jonathan got to the letter D, Elizabeth had wrapped a pillow around her head. She whirled around and faced the corner. She waited a good long time, then slowly turned her head. Peter and Jonathan stood in the middle of the room, grinning.

"Are you *done*, Jonathan?"

"Yeah, but I could start again."

"Well, I'm calling a case meeting," said Elizabeth quickly. "And . . . uh . . . this can be our headquarters." She plopped down on a large gray rug in the middle of the wooden floor. The two boys sat across from her.

"I don't think this is a very good case," said Jonathan. "We're never gonna find out who the mystery man is. And Edna's going to be really sad 'cause everyone will still think her grandmother stole the scroll."

Elizabeth opened her notebook and stared at her page of clues. It *seemed* like the mystery man with the fever had confessed to stealing the Chinese scroll. But how could they prove it if they didn't even know his name?

"I say, if I just had my computer," said Peter. "Maybe I could . . ."

Elizabeth shook her head. "I don't think your computer could help us. We don't know very much. Just that the

24

mystery man had a fever in 1890 and called out for someone named Rebecca. And he knew about Stone Harbor."

Elizabeth stretched over to the night table and picked up a thick leather-bound book. *How to Think Like a Detective.* "This is what we need."

Jonathan, as usual, took one look at the book and tried to escape, but she clamped her hand on his arm.

"If you get bossy and read that book out loud," said Jonathan, "I'm gonna start eructating again."

"I'm not going to read it out loud, and anyway I don't know why you're so allergic to my book. It just says there's always more than one path to the truth. If you can't get through one way, you have to find another."

"I don't get it."

"So we forget about the mystery man for now. And we try and find a copy of that history book that was stolen. If someone doesn't want Hattie and Edna to read *The History of Stone Harbor*, that could mean there's a clue in it."

"I also am having an idea," said Peter. "We must catch this person who stole the letter and also the history book from Hattie and Edna's house."

"I don't know," said Elizabeth. "The door was unlocked for half an hour. Anyone could have walked in, or even just reached in through the window."

"But I am suspecting someone." Peter's eyes had turned bright and eager, like the beady eyes of a ferret, Elizabeth thought. He continued. "I suspect the library lady."

"The librarian?" Elizabeth looked down at her notes. Mildred Patterson. Edna *did* tell her about the letter, and the librarian was outside the house just before the letter disappeared. But she looked so nice. And librarians don't go around stealing things.

"Look here, chaps," said Peter. "We must shadow this library lady everywhere." He began pacing around the room. "We must be spies. We must follow her every move. We must . . ." The look on Elizabeth's face stopped him. "We must . . . maybe not be spies. But we will set – how do you call it? – a trap for the person who stole the letter." Elizabeth groaned. Not another one of Peter's traps. "We will get in no trouble of course," he added.

"News update!" Mr. Pollack appeared at the top of the spiral staircase. "I just ran into Hattie at the store. She had something very interesting to say. You know how the mystery man kept muttering about looking at the sea. Out past Stone Harbor. Now she remembers. He said it had to be done by the light of the full moon."

"The full moon?" asked Jonathan. "How come?"

"I have no idea," said Mr. Pollack. "But I do know one thing – it just so happens that tomorrow night the moon will be full." Elizabeth looked out the window. "Too bad we can't see the harbor from here."

Mr. Pollack smiled. "Oh, that's no problem. Hattie knows of a place where you can get a perfect view of the harbor. The highest spot in town. She's already made all the arrangements."

"Great!" said Elizabeth. "Where?"

"You'll be going to an old inn."

"An old . . . inn?" Elizabeth straightened up. It couldn't be the spooky old place on the edge of town. That one was empty. No one would want to go there.

"It has a name you can't forget," said Mr. Pollack. He leaned forward and widened his eyes. "The Jeremiah Coffin Inn."

The Investigation Begins

At Rosewood Cottage the next morning, Elizabeth sat down with the others at the round table, her mind still on the Jeremiah Coffin Inn. She imagined the creaky hallways and dark rooms. The thought of being in there at night . . .

"Wild blueberry soup," announced Edna. She brought in bowls of warm blueberries with a spot of whipped cream on top. Jonathan and Peter dug in as if they didn't have a care in the world. Daisy, all eyebrows and whiskers, sat in the doorway looking like a shaggy old sea captain.

"Hattie," said Elizabeth. "My dad thought you said we're going to the Jeremiah Coffin Inn tonight. But that place is empty." She waited for Hattie to tell her that Mr. Pollack had misunderstood.

"That's right!" bubbled Hattie. "See, we need to be up high. The mystery man said to look out beyond the harbor on the night of the full moon. Oh, you'll get a dandy view from the top floor of the inn."

"But, I mean, we can't just go in there, can we?"

Edna patted Elizabeth's hand. "Don't worry about that. Tom has the key. Hattie's nephew. He said he would come over this morning and drop it off."

"You see, my sister and her husband ran the inn for years," explained Hattie. "They retired, oh, about three years ago. Their son Tom hasn't had a bit of luck sellin' the place for them. I just can't fathom why no one is interested."

"Maybe people think it's haunted," said Jonathan. "Because of that name – Coffin."

Hattie smiled. "Oh, Coffin is a good old Yankee name. But as far as ghost stories, you're right. There *is* talk of a ghost – what you might call the town ghost. He was a one-legged pirate, Mad Dan Hawkins. Folks say the inn was built on the very spot where he buried his pirate treasure. They say he comes back at night to look for it. Walks up and down the halls with his wooden crutch thumping on the floor." Hattie added another dab of whipped cream to her bowl. "Course I don't believe foolish talk like that. Bunch o' flapdoodle, if you ask me."

Jonathan split the air with a karate chop. "No problem. I'm not afraid of ghosts."

The others laughed, but Elizabeth didn't say anything. She didn't believe in ghosts. But still, she was glad she wouldn't be wandering around the empty old inn by herself.

"How about if we meet there at . . ." Hattie was interrupted by a light tap at the window. A face with a trim gray beard peered through the glass. "Come on in, Tom," she called. "The door isn't locked."

Daisy gave a few barks at the sound of footsteps in the hall, but squirmed in delight as soon as she saw who it was. Hattie's nephew walked into the room and slid into a chair next to his aunt. He was short like Hattie, and restless with energy even when he was sitting down.

"Sorry, Aunt Hattie. I don't have much time. I just wanted to drop off these keys on my way out of town." He put his arm around Hattie's shoulder. "You were very mysterious on the phone about why you want these. But something tells me it has to do with that missing scroll you're looking for."

"It's just a clue we're following up on," said Hattie. "A long shot, you might say." She took the bundle of keys from her nephew and introduced him to the Three-Star Detectives.

"Just be careful. There's no power in the building. So no lights." Tom got up to leave. "I'll be in Bangor for a week. I'll call as soon as I get back." He brushed Hattie's forehead with a kiss then hurried out of the room.

At the sound of the front door closing, Edna turned to the others. "So how about starting our case meeting? I can't wait to hear what the Three-Star Detectives came up with."

Peter popped up from his chair. "The Case of the Chinese Scroll," he announced. "Now I am thinking . . ."

"Uh . . . Peter? I wrote down the ideas. Remember?" Elizabeth opened her notebook as Peter sat down.

"In honor of our guest from Germany," she said, "I'll mention Peter's idea first. He thinks we need to find out who stole the letter and the history book. And that we should set a trap for the thief. He'll work out more details later."

Hattie rubbed her hands together. "This is just like old times! Too bad no one uses hair grease anymore!"

Elizabeth looked down at her notebook. "My idea is about the old history book. Someone took Edna's copy, and probably the two copies from the Spencer Library. I think that means there's a clue in the book. About who the mystery man is. So we need to get a copy of *The History of Stone Harbor*. And fast. The person who took the books and the letter may be looking for the scroll too."

"You're right," said Edna. "Of course, I did look at the book, and I didn't see any clue. Then again, my detective skills are a little rusty. Now let's see. As far as finding the book, that may not be so easy. It's not being printed any more. Our library could borrow it from another library, but that could take a long time. Maybe we . . ."

"The Treasure Barn!" bellowed Hattie.

"Good gracious, you practically scared me to death," laughed Edna. "But it *is* a good idea. The Treasure Barn has got just about everything under the sun."

"It's up on Route One, about five miles north," said Hattie. "They've got every kind of junk you can think of. And a whole room full of old books. They might have a copy of *The History of Stone Harbor*. It's worth a try."

As Elizabeth wrote down the information, Edna straightened herself in her chair. "Hattie and I came up with a few ideas ourselves. Haven't had much luck though. First of all, we searched the house again. Top to bottom. The letter and the history book aren't here, that's for sure. And we called Hattie's friend. We asked her to look for more pages of the letter about the mystery man. No luck there either. That was the only page."

Elizabeth closed her notebook. "Well, I guess for now we have to try and get *The History of Stone Harbor* and see if it gives us a clue."

Hattie and Edna walked them to the door. "And don't forget about tonight," said Hattie. "Let's meet in front of the inn. Better wait until it's good and dark. Say 10:30."

The three detectives took the beach path back to the house.

"My parents will take us to this . . . this Treasure Barn," said Peter. "They are liking this kind of thing." Peter was right. He easily persuaded his parents, promising them rooms full of strange items.

They set out late in the afternoon, winding past rocky fields and quiet coves. Elizabeth looked out the window, trying to pick out her favorite house. At first she chose a stately old mansion with a sweeping front porch, but then she saw a sunny little cottage with the sea at its doorstep and a garden of bright flowers.

After they reached the busy highway, their destination was easy to spot. A wooden sign shaped like a hand pointed to an enormous white barn. *If you can't find it here*, read the letters on the sign, *you probably don't need it*. A large open doorway led to a place crammed with treasures from top to bottom. Wooden cigar boxes, rusty wagons, jukeboxes, wind-up toys. Even an ancient wooden sleigh.

While Peter's parents admired an old barber chair, Elizabeth asked for the used books. A young woman directed the three detectives upstairs to a cavernous room smelling of dust and dry paper. Long tables, piled high with books, filled the room.

"The lady said the books about Maine are at the far end," said Jonathan. "Under the . . . Oh, no." Jonathan pointed to the other side of the room. Mr. and Mrs. Edmond were there, looking through the books on a table marked *Local History*.

"I can't believe they're here," whispered Elizabeth. "I hope they're not looking for the same book we are."

Elizabeth didn't dare move closer. The Edmonds were sending a double scowl in their direction.

"What are we going to do?"

Jonathan tugged Peter's arm. "Sing," he commanded.

"Hold on, old chap. You said you get . . . how is it called . . . sick at your stomach when I sing."

"That's okay. Just sing. Loud."

Peter raised one arm, strolling toward the Edmonds as he sang in his heavy German accent. "A fair maiden sat blushing by the babbling brook, the babbling brook, oh, the babbling brook." Peter clasped his hands over his heart. He turned up the volume. "Let us plight our troth, said the golden haired lad. Yes, plight our troth. Oh, plight our troth." Peter took a deep breath, getting ready for the part about the orb of love hanging lonely in the sky. But the Edmonds were slowly backing out the door, as if they were escaping from a growling dog.

Elizabeth rushed to the table. "Let's hurry up before they complain to the owner." Jonathan and Peter started at opposite ends of the table. Elizabeth shuffled through the pile of books in the middle. Walking tours of Maine. Legends of New England. A book about bridges. One about lighthouses. Sailing ships. Lobsters.

"I got it!" shouted Jonathan. He held up an old book with a torn dust jacket. "And it only costs a dollar." Elizabeth pulled four quarters out of her pocket as they headed to the stairs. She got halfway down, then stopped. The Edmonds were down below, standing by the door. Elizabeth turned around and shooed the boys back upstairs.

"We have to wait until they're gone," she whispered. A few minutes later, with the Edmonds nowhere in sight, she rushed downstairs and stood in line to pay. Peter appeared in line behind her. He had found a second copy of the book and was getting ready to buy it.

"Peter, what's going on? How come you're buying another copy?" Peter only smiled and shrugged his shoulders. "On second thought," muttered Elizabeth, "maybe I don't want to know."

Elizabeth settled onto a bench in front of the building. Carefully, she turned the stiff dry pages. When she found the paragraph that discussed the theft, the boys read over her shoulder.

"It just the same stuff we already know," said Jonathan. "About the sea captain getting the scroll in China. And how someone stole it from the town hall in 1890."

Elizabeth reread the paragraph. "Well, it does tell us a little more about the scroll. It was a small scroll painted during the . . ." She looked down at the book again. "During the Sung Dynasty. It shows a plum tree in bloom. And there's some writing in the corner of the scroll. And the sea captain who gave the scroll to the town was named John Morgridge."

Peter's parents walked up to them, smiling. "We buy a true piece of America," announced Herr Hoffmann. Proudly, he held out his purchase – a birdhouse painted like a barber shop.

Elizabeth sat quietly on the way home. She had been certain the history book would give them a clue. Now she wasn't so sure. But if there wasn't a clue, why did someone want to keep Hattie and Edna from having the book?

Back at the house, Elizabeth had little time to think about the mystery. She called Edna and Hattie to tell them about the book. After that, she and Jonathan helped with the special going-away dinner. Peter's parents would be leaving the next day for a two-week tour of science libraries.

"Excuse me. Dinner's ready." Elizabeth stood by the closed door to Peter's bedroom. She could hear muffled voices speaking in German. Peter's parents planned to leave early the next morning. They were having one last serious talk with their son. Elizabeth could imagine Peter making solemn promises to be on his best behavior.

After dinner, they played a lively game of charades. Peter raced from room to room, swaying like a gorilla. "*Planet of the Apes!*" cried Mr. Pollack.

Just after ten o'clock, Peter's watch began a set of quick beeps. The talking and laughing stopped. Elizabeth had pushed away the thought of the Jeremiah Coffin Inn. Now there was no forgetting. The time for games was over.

The three detectives changed into warm clothes and hunted for their flashlights. Shortly before 10:30 Elizabeth grabbed her detective notebook and climbed into the car with Mrs. Pollack and the boys. She thought about last summer, when she and Jonathan had a midnight adventure at another abandoned building. It had given her the fright of her life. But tonight everything was different, she told herself. Completely different.

The trip to the inn went more quickly than Elizabeth would have liked. She took her time getting out of the car.

"Hey, we're gonna lose the moon!" Jonathan pointed to a black cloud, sweeping across the sky like a pirate ship at full sail. Within seconds the moonlight disappeared behind its dark bulk.

Elizabeth stood on the sidewalk, not ready to walk away from the car. The Jeremiah Coffin Inn was gloomy enough during the day. But now, in the black of night, it looked positively . . . ghostly.

A Fright at the Inn

Mrs. Pollack rolled down her window. "I could come with you, if you'd like."

"Oh. Uh . . . Well . . ." Elizabeth couldn't picture Sherlock Holmes having his mother come along. "I think we'll be all right." She pointed to two figures making their way down the road. "Hattie and Edna are here. And Rosewood Cottage is just down the street. We'll go back there and call you when we're done."

"Okay. I get the message. Just make sure to keep an eye on Jonathan. Don't let him wander."

Hattie and Edna arrived a few seconds later, lighting up the night in lemon yellow warm-up suits.

"Nothing like a mystery to make you feel young again," said Edna. She adjusted a gauzy scarf protecting her hairdo.

Hattie rattled the bundle of keys Tom had given her. "We're all set. We'll have to go in the back way though."

"My good lady," said Peter, springing into the lead, "I light the way with my new flashlight." Elizabeth only half listened as Peter described his flashlight. Super-duper mega ultra high-intensity. Or something like that. She frowned as she turned on her own flashlight. She had forgotten to change the batteries and it was already flickering.

Jonathan and Elizabeth walked with Edna, who felt her way carefully with her cane. The group stayed close to the side of the house, well away from the edge of the bluff. At the back of the inn, they reached a cement terrace. Even in the dark, Elizabeth could feel the power of the ocean below. The waves swelled up and rumbled against the shore, like a giant taking long, deep breaths.

Hattie stood at the wide back door, trying the keys one by one. The last key produced a sharp click. Without a sound, the door swung open. Hattie turned to the others. "Looks like the house is invitin' us to come in."

"A jolly good start," said Peter. "Maybe we meet that pirate chap tonight."

Elizabeth managed a weak laugh. She bent down for a moment to tie her shoe, then hurried to catch up with the others. They had stepped into an enormous kitchen, brightly lit by Peter's flashlight.

"Follow me," said Hattie. "And stay together." They walked in single file, making their way into a long parlor. The room was bare except for a dark clump of furniture at the very center, where a sofa and four armchairs had been pushed together. Hattie led them into the front hallway, then stopped at the foot of the stairs.

"Edna can't do the stairs," she said. "So I'll stay down here with her. We can see the ocean out the dining room window. Course the best view is upstairs."

"Oh, yes," said Peter. "We like the best view."

"Then you youngsters go all the way up to the third floor," said Hattie. "There's a room right at the top of the stairs. Let's just hope the moon decides to come out from behind that cloud." She and Edna walked around the corner into the dining room.

Elizabeth started up the stairs. "Wait! My notebook! I left it outside when I tied my shoe." She started to ask Jonathan to go back with her, but she stopped herself. The truth was, she was afraid of the dark. But she wasn't going to admit that to Peter.

"You two stay here," she said. "And *don't* go upstairs without me." Clicking on her flashlight, she rushed through the parlor and into the kitchen. Without giving herself time to think, she sprinted out the door and scooped up the notebook. As she hurried back into the kitchen, the cloud slipped away. The moonlight came on strong, throwing a frosty gleam onto the white walls. Elizabeth stepped easily across the bright kitchen, but the dark entry to the parlor stopped her. With the curtains drawn tight, the room was as black as a cave. She listened for the reassuring sound of voices but heard only the lonely rolling of the sea.

Elizabeth held the flashlight with two hands, squeezing hard. She pushed forward. Walk straight ahead, she told herself. Don't look into the dark corners. And don't stop. She could see the outline of the couch now. She was almost to the middle of the room.

As Elizabeth passed the couch, something brushed against her foot. With a cry of surprise, she jerked her leg back. Too late. She was in the iron grip of a hand – a hand that had snaked out of the darkness and wrapped itself around her ankle.

A blast of terror shot through her body and came out as a scream. An instant later something popped up from behind the couch. Jonathan!

"I'm sorry, Elizabeth! Sorry! Stop screaming."

Peter ran into the room, with Hattie and Edna following. Jonathan hopped from one foot to the other, talking fast. "I thought she would know it was me. I . . . kind of . . . hid behind the couch and grabbed her foot."

Elizabeth stood with her arms crossed. She held herself tight, as if her body might fly apart. "You are the worst brother in the whole world," she hissed. "And forget about the Three-Star Detective Agency. It's hereby . . . hereby . . . out of business." Edna led Elizabeth to the couch and sat down with her. "Now, you just sit down here for a minute, Elizabeth. Get over the shock. Hattie, open the curtains, please."

Hattie parted the heavy curtains and let in a bright patch of moonlight.

"We've got to remember why we're here," said Edna softly. She turned to Jonathan. "This isn't a game. We're ace detectives, all of us. And we're trying to prove that the mystery man, not my grandmother, stole the Chinese scroll. We've got to do just like the mystery man said – look out past the harbor by the light of the full moon. See if it's some kind of clue about where the scroll is hidden."

"That's right," said Hattie. "And I'm sure we won't have any more foolish tricks."

Elizabeth looked down at Jonathan. He had melted into a miserable heap, sitting on the floor with his hands over his eyes. "Sorry, Elizabeth. Really. I didn't know you'd get so scared." His voice slid into a sob.

Elizabeth felt her anger soften. Jonathan was about as annoying as a brother could be. But she couldn't stand to see him cry. Sometimes she felt as if they were connected by an invisible string. When he cried, she could feel the string pulling against her.

"Okay, Jon. Just forget it. I'm not mad anymore."

"Good show!" said Peter. "Jolly decent of you, Elizabeth."

He helped Jonathan off the floor and clapped him on the back. "And now, my good fellow, we go back to our mystery."

"All right," said Hattie. "Let's start over again. You three head up to the room at the top of the stairs. Third floor. Let's take a look before any more clouds cover up the moon." She and Edna returned to the dining room.

Peter walked up the stairs first, lighting up a wide carpeted stairway. On the second floor, the carpet ended. A set of bare wooden steps led to the top floor.

As soon as they reached the third floor, Elizabeth squeezed past the boys. She didn't want Peter to think she was scared. Especially after her scream in the parlor.

"I'll go first." Elizabeth crossed the hallway and pulled open a door. She had prepared herself for an empty room. Instead, the place was neatly arranged with furniture, looking cold and pale in the moonlight. In the corner, an old-fashioned canopy bed wore a fancy patchwork quilt, as if guests would be arriving at any moment.

"Turn your flashlight off, Peter. So we can see the moon better." Elizabeth was drawn to a pair of large windows facing the sea. Hattie was right. The view was perfect. The moon had risen high, crisp against the dark sky. A few boats bobbed in the harbor. Just beyond, where the moonlight touched the water, a wide glittering path stretched out to the open sea.

"And now," commanded Peter. "We must think of the words of the mystery man. The words spoken in his fever." Peter found a beam of moonlight and stood like an actor on center stage. "Look out to sea," he murmured. "Beyond Stone Harbor, by the light of the full moon." He tossed his head feverishly. "Out to sea. Out to sea. Beyond Stone Harbor, by the . . ."

"Okay, Peter. We get it."

Elizabeth stood at the window with the boys behind her. She squinted into the distance, following the sparkling ribbon of moonlight until it met the black edge of the sky. Moonlight on the sea. Beyond the harbor. So beautiful. But what did it have to do with their mystery?

"I don't know," she said. "What if this doesn't have anything to do with the scroll? Maybe the mystery man was talking about something completely different and . . ." Elizabeth stopped at the sound of a deep, mumbling voice.

"Peter, you're going to scare me to death. Just quit acting weird." She whirled around. But Peter, and Jonathan too, were silent, looking wide-eyed and worried.

Elizabeth turned her eyes to the open doorway. She could hear something else now. A shuffling on the stairs.

One heavy footstep, and then – the sound of wood on wood. Step. Thump. Step. Thump. Again, the mumbling voice, getting louder and closer. Elizabeth didn't believe in ghosts, but how could she not think it? Mad Dan, the one-legged pirate!

"I say," quivered Peter. "I say." At that point he began muttering to himself in German.

Elizabeth stared at the open door. If only she could work up the courage to close it. Put something between them and whatever was coming up the stairs. She took one brave, trembling step forward. Before she could come any closer, the door was banged shut from the outside.

Elizabeth jumped back and found herself sandwiched between Peter and Jonathan. She could hear footsteps pounding down the stairs. Then, silence. Peter crept up to the door and turned the knob. The door wouldn't open. They were locked in!

"*Hilfe!*" he shouted. "*Hilfe! Wir sind eingesperrt!*"[3]

"We're locked in!" yelled Jonathan.

"It's okay. Nothin' to worry about." It was Hattie's voice, coming from far below.

"Someone was up here!" yelled Elizabeth.

"Don't worry. I'm coming. It'll take me awhile though." Slow footsteps shuffled up the stairs.

Finally, they could hear Hattie's voice close-by. "The door doesn't lock from the outside," she said. "It must be stuck. All right, now you push and I'll pull." A moment later the door flew open with a jerk.

"I say," said Peter, "that was a bit of fun." Elizabeth rolled her eyes. Peter had found his courage again. And his English.

"What was it?" Jonathan's voice was still shaky.

---

[3] HILL-feh. Veer zint EIN-ge-shpairt. "Help. We're locked in!"

39

"It wasn't the ghost of old Mad Dan, I'll tell you that much," said Hattie. "It was some dang fool running down the stairs with a broom. Came right past Edna and me. Might have been a fella. We couldn't see the face though." She gave a satisfied chuckle. "If you ask me, I think we scared him half to death. He lit out the back door runnin' like greased lightning."

When they reached the bottom of the stairs they found Edna nervously twisting a small handkerchief. "Thank goodness you children are all right." She turned to Hattie. "I think you have to admit something strange is going on. Somebody is trying to stop us from working on this case. Stealing the letter and the history books, and now trying to scare us." She dabbed at her nose with a handkerchief. "Maybe we're too old to be chasing after mysteries."

"Now let's just keep our wits about us," said Hattie. "No reason to panic. If you ask me, this was more like a silly prank. We may be eighty years old, Edna, but we've still got some weasel juice left in us. No need to give up a case just because some fool clomps around with a broom."

Peter clapped. "Well said, my good lady."

"All right," said Hattie. "We've all had time to look at the moonlight on the harbor. Better lock up the house and get out of here. But first . . . does the Three-Star Detective Agency stay on the case?" Peter gave a thumbs up sign. Then Jonathan. Then Elizabeth.

"And the Baker Street Girls?" added Hattie.

Edna hesitated, then gave a determined tap with her cane. "Case meeting tomorrow at Rosewood Cottage," she said. "Ten o'clock. Refreshments will be served."

The Storyteller's Clue

By the time Elizabeth slipped into bed, it was nearly midnight. The moonlight poured through the roof window, painting a pale square of white onto the foot of the bed. Elizabeth's body ached for sleep, but her mind gave her no rest. First the old letter and the history book had disappeared. Then two more copies of the book were missing from the library in Spencer. And now this prank. Edna was right. Someone didn't want them working on the case.

Not that they were making any progress. They hadn't figured out if there was a clue in the history book. Or if the moonlight shining on the sea had anything to do with the stolen scroll. And now, after tonight, she was sure their parents wouldn't let them go out after dark. Elizabeth puffed up her pillow for the third time. It wasn't easy being an eleven-year-old detective.

As soon as she woke up in the morning, Elizabeth felt the warm touch of sunlight on her face. She jumped out of bed and looked out the window. The sea was a restless blue, with waves chopping the water into little peaks.

"Good morning." Mrs. Pollack's voice came from the kitchen.

Elizabeth padded down the spiral staircase and glanced at the clock. "Mom, how come you let me sleep so long? We wanted to go to Rosewood Cottage this morning." Elizabeth hurried into the kitchen, pouring cereal into a bowl as she stumbled along. She wasn't happy when she heard that Peter and Jonathan were already gone. Peter had gotten up early to say good-bye to his parents. After Jonathan got up, the two went to look for clues outside the inn. Without her.

"You needed to sleep, and I told them not to wake you." Mrs. Pollack took a cup of coffee and sat down with

Elizabeth at the table. "You know, last night you said you didn't see any clue in the moonlight shining on the sea. But I was just thinking. Maybe you weren't supposed to. Looking out to sea by the light of the full moon. It sounds like some kind of legend to me. Maybe that's where the clue is. In the legend."

Elizabeth, still crunching her cereal, gave a nod.

"The newspaper says a storyteller is coming to the library this morning," continued Mrs. Pollack. "At eleven o'clock. Why don't you go there and talk to him? Storytellers are good memory keepers. He must know lots of forgotten tales. Maybe he knows a story about moonlight on the harbor."

Elizabeth grabbed her detective notebook as she slipped into her shoes. "Sure, Mom. Thanks. But I gotta go."

"Don't forget," called Mr. Pollack after her. "Harbor-fest is today. Right on Main Street. We'll meet you and the boys there at noon for lunch."

Elizabeth hurried along the beach toward Stone Harbor. In the distance loomed the Jeremiah Coffin Inn, still keeping a lonely watch high above the sea.

At Rosewood Cottage Hattie opened the door. "You're just in time," she said. "Peter and Jonathan got here a few minutes ago."

Jonathan and Edna sat in the front room. Peter, dressed in his white lab coat, hovered over the round table with a mad scientist gleam in his eye. He waved his hand. "Stay back! Don't touch the evidence."

Elizabeth looked down. On the table was a straw broom with a red handle.

"They found it in the bushes near the inn," said Edna. "That's what was making the thumping noise on the stairs."

"You observe my technique, please." Peter pushed up his sleeves and wiggled his fingers. Daisy was ordered into the corner. With a pudgy brush from his detective case, Peter dusted black powder along the handle. "Hmm. Well . . ." He brushed more powder. "Rotten luck, chaps," he said. "Nothing but smears."

Elizabeth didn't say anything. She wondered if Peter had ever actually found a fingerprint. She had never seen him get anything but smears.

"I know," said Jonathan. "We could go to the store and see who bought a broom like this."

"There's only one problem," said Hattie. She walked out of the room and returned with a straw broom identical to the one on the table. "Stone Harbor is a small town. Only one hardware store. Every Tom, Dick, and Harry has the same broom. And another thing about a small town. Everybody knows everyone else's business. Could be a lot of people knew we were going to the inn last night."

"No matter," said Peter. "I have other ideas. Good ideas. I have been doing much thinking." He gave a megawatt smile that chilled Elizabeth to the bone. She could almost see the word *trouble* light up like a neon sign.

Jonathan looked at Edna. "I thought we were going to have something to . . ." Elizabeth gave him a light kick under the table, but he continued. "Ow . . . Something to eat. Remember when you said *refreshments will be served*?"

Elizabeth glared at him. "You're so rude," she mouthed.

Edna shuffled out of the room. "Oh, my. I almost forgot. And Daisy's alone in the kitchen." She came back with pieces of toast topped with cream cheese and a circle of raisins. Daisy appeared in the doorway with suspicious clumps of white in her whiskers.

"Time to clear the evidence off the table," said Hattie. She set the broom in the corner and passed around the plates. "Now I'm burnin' to talk about last night. So how about it? Why did the mystery man say to look out to sea in the moonlight. Did anyone figure out the clue?" Elizabeth

43

opened her detective notebook to a page headed *Clue of the Full Moon*. It was blank. "I couldn't think of a thing," she said. One by one, the others shook their heads. The moonlit scene seemed to have nothing to do with the stolen scroll.

"At least we have the book now," said Elizabeth. "*The History of Stone Harbor*. I haven't found any clue yet. But it might be there somewhere."

"If only we knew who's trying to stop us," said Edna. "I have a feeling that person knows something important about the mystery. Something we don't know. Too bad it was so dark last night. The person ran right past us, and we couldn't see a thing."

Peter leaned forward eagerly. "See here, chaps. We must set a trap for this villain. And this shall be our . . . how do you call it? . . . bait." He opened his detective case and pulled out his copy of *The History of Stone Harbor*.

Hattie's eyes lit up. "I'll tell you one thing. This is a good day for settin' traps. Harborfest starts at noon. Everyone in town will be there."

Elizabeth looked at her watch and closed her notebook. "Sorry. I have to go. There's a storyteller coming to the library. Mom thought he might be able to help us. He might know a legend about looking out to sea in the moonlight." She turned to go. "Anybody interested?"

Elizabeth didn't wait for an answer. The others huddled around Peter, hatching some plot. Hattie and Edna were giggling. Daisy sneaked out of the room with Peter's fingerprint brush in her mouth.

Elizabeth let herself out the front door and walked across the street to the library. In the cozy main room, a group of young children sat squirming on the floor in front of a large fireplace. Elizabeth looked around, feeling a blush explode across her face. The oldest member of the audience was about seven years old. Why did she let her mother talk her into this? She started to back up, but it was too late to escape. A round little man strode past her into the room. Elizabeth pulled up a chair and sat in back with the parents.

The storyteller squeezed himself into a creaky rocking chair. He sat silently for a moment, stroking a white beard that plunged halfway down his chest. Finally he leaned forward. "Edward Harrington," he announced. "Teller of tales." Story hour had begun.

"Now, the population of the state o' Maine is over one million," he began. "But that's just during the day. At night the population pretty near doubles in size. Gets awful crowded around here." He rocked forward and stopped. His brown eyes narrowed into slits. "That's when the ghosts come back."

For the next hour, one story followed another. Ghost pirates guarding secret treasure. Skeletons dancing in the churchyard. Haunted islands. Sunken ships. The storyteller's voice rose and fell like waves on the sea. Sometimes it was so deep and quiet Elizabeth had to lean forward to hear. Then, without warning, the voice would blare like a foghorn. By the time he finished, only the bravest children remained on the floor. The rest were huddled on laps.

Elizabeth stayed as the others filed out. Mr. Harrington leaned back in the rocking chair and closed his eyes. Elizabeth tiptoed up to him.

"Excuse me," she said softly. "I was wondering if you could help me with something."

Mr. Harrington's eyes fluttered open. He looked up at her. "Well, I'll see what I can do."

"It's about . . . about a person who lived a long time ago. He said something about looking out to sea. Beyond Stone Harbor. And it had to be done by the light of the full moon. I was just wondering. Could that be some kind of legend?"

Mr. Harrington rocked back and forth in the chair. He closed his eyes as he folded his meaty hands over his stomach. Elizabeth was afraid he had fallen asleep. "That does sound familiar," he said, opening his eyes. "You see, I've been writing down old sea shanties – sailor's songs – for years now. So they don't disappear."

A memory keeper, thought Elizabeth. Just like her mother had thought.

"And I heard something like that in a song." He stopped talking. "Look out to the open sea," he said after a long silence. "Look out beyond Stone Harbor by the light of the full moon, and you'll see the ghost ships."

"The what?"

"The ghost ships. Ships that have sunk. Now, according to the song, the ghost ships sail past Stone Harbor when the full moon shines on the sea. Like a parade of sunken ships. That's all I know about the story." He began to hum as he rocked back and forth. Then he sang, his voice quivering just above a whisper.

"*When the moon is full, with their ghostly crews, the ships rise up from the sea. They'll be sailin' soon, by the light of the moon, and as cold as stone they will be.*"

Mrs. Patterson, the librarian, appeared from behind a row of bookshelves. "Harborfest is getting started," she said. "I'll be locking up the library."

Elizabeth thanked Mr. Harrington and walked away. A sailor's song. So the mystery man was probably someone who had gone to sea. It was only a small clue, but better than nothing.

For a moment Elizabeth stood outside the library. The morning had ripened into a golden summer day. She stood in the sun, letting it melt away the tales of ghosts and goblins. The Harborfest was already in full swing. The hard-working fishing boats rested in the harbor. A small parade was just ending. Where the main street was closed off, a line of tables offered children's games and craft sales.

46

Elizabeth spotted her parents sitting at a picnic table set up in the street. Jonathan and Peter sat next to them, talking to Hattie and Edna.

"Peter won the watermelon seed spitting contest," announced Jonathan.

"And Mr. Edmond ended up with the booby prize," laughed Hattie. "Got too close to the line of fire. Ended up with a watermelon seed in his mustache!"

Elizabeth sat down at the picnic table. "Well, I've got some news too!" She turned to Mrs. Pollack. "You were right about the storyteller, Mom. He knew a song about looking out to sea in the moonlight." Elizabeth told them about the sunken ships coming back to Stone Harbor as ghost ships. "If the mystery man knew that song, he was probably a sailor who came from Stone Harbor. So now we know one more thing about him."

Peter and Jonathan didn't seem impressed. They stared at a large canvas tote bag sitting on a nearby table.

"I don't think you even heard what I said," sniffed Elizabeth. "And what are you two staring at, anyway?"

"Our trap," whispered Jonathan. Elizabeth got up and walked past the bag. She could see a book sticking out of the top. The title was in plain sight – *The History of Stone Harbor*. Now she understood. Three copies of the history book had disappeared. If the thief tried to steal this one, they would be ready.

Jonathan nudged her as she sat down at the table. "The librarian. Look what she's doing." Mrs. Patterson stood in front of the library. She seemed to be staring at the canvas bag. Slowly she began walking toward it. A sudden commotion stopped her.

"Now, how did you get that door open? You just stay there!" Elizabeth turned her head at the sound of Hattie's voice. The door to Rosewood Cottage stood open, and a little gray face peered out. Hattie hurried toward the cottage, but

Daisy had already bolted out. The tiny schnauzer turned and faced the crowd, her long whiskers quivering. She barked in all directions, jumping up and down like a wind-up toy.

Suddenly her bark became a growl. Elizabeth followed the dog's gaze and found herself looking at Mr. Edmond. She gulped. Mr. Edmond, unlucky as usual, was wearing plaid pants.

"I say, my dear chap," called Peter. "This dog is not liking plaid pants. You must watch your backseat!"

Mr. Edmond took a step back as Daisy began to charge. Then, spotting the book sticking out of the canvas bag, he grabbed *The History of Stone Harbor*. Holding out the book like a shield, he swatted at Daisy. Hattie rushed over and scooped up the dog.

"This is an outrage!" snapped Mr. Edmond. "Are you the owner of this creature?" He placed the book on a picnic table.

"You know very well I am," said Hattie. "And I'm sorry she ran at you like that. Course, far as I can see, there's been no harm done." Daisy barked in agreement. "We don't let her run loose. Not ordinarily. Can't help it if she gets out once in a while."

Daisy's escape seemed to be the main event of the day. The woman doing face painting stopped what she was doing. The juggler dropped one of the pie pans he was balancing. Daisy completed the act by wriggling out of Hattie's arms and snatching a hot dog off Edna's plate.

"Show's over, folks!" said Hattie as she got hold of the dog again. She lifted Daisy's paw and made it wave to the crowd. A few people clapped. Elizabeth turned to Peter. She was surprised to see him slumped on a bench, with his head in his hands. "*O nein!*"[4] he mumbled. "Dash it all!"

---

[4] *Nein* means *no* and is pronounced like the number *nine*.

"What's wrong, Peter? Don't worry about the book. You can just put it back in the bag. Then the trap will be set again."

"I know, but . . . this Mr. Edmond chap. He touched the book. He will have a problem." Peter pointed to the palm of his hand.

Elizabeth felt her stomach drop to her feet. "Peter! You didn't use staining powder!" She motioned for Jonathan to come over.

Without a word, Peter took a small bottle out of his pocket. Elizabeth recognized the powder at once. Anything it touched would turn bright purple. He had used it last summer in Germany when they worked on their first case together. And they had gotten into plenty of trouble.

"Sorry, chaps. I wanted to make sure we catch the thief. I sprinkled powder on the cover of the book. So when the thief takes the book, the hand turns purple."

Jonathan groaned. "How long do we have?"

"I use only the best instant-action powder," said Peter. "Mr. Edmond's hands. They will be purple now."

Elizabeth looked over at her parents, who were standing in line at one of the food tables. "Get ready for Lecture Number Nineteen," she said. "*You kids have gone too far!*"

A Ghostly Clue

"You kids have gone too far!" Mrs. Pollack stood with Jonathan and Elizabeth at the edge of the crowd. Her words poured out in an angry whisper. Mr. Pollack and Peter were in front of the library with Mr. Edmond. He attacked his purple hands with a large handkerchief.

"But, Mom," said Jonathan. "We were just trying to trap the thief. Peter didn't tell us he was going to use staining powder. Really."

"That may be. But you . . . I don't know. You encourage him." Mrs. Pollack stared straight ahead, pressing her mouth together so tight, her lips disappeared.

Elizabeth looked over at Rosewood Cottage. Hattie and Edna had taken Daisy inside. The dog was probably getting a stern lecture too.

Peter and Mr. Pollack returned. No relief in sight, thought Elizabeth. Her father's face glowed like hot charcoal.

"It's going to take days for that stain to wear off Mr. Edmond's hands," he snapped. "I'll just say one thing. Case or no case, this kind of behavior has to stop. Otherwise we'll have to call Peter's parents." He handed Peter a piece of newspaper. "Wrap up that book and make sure no one else touches it." Peter nodded and hurried over to pick up the book.

The group sat at the picnic table and had a somber lunch. Jonathan and Peter silently worked their way through an order of fried clams. Elizabeth eyed a pot of boiling water next to a barrel crawling with lobsters. She decided to have a pizza slice.

As soon as lunch was over, the family walked back to the vacation house.

"I'm not sure if you'll be allowed to keep working on this case," said Mr. Pollack as they walked in the door. "Your mother and I will have to talk."

Elizabeth glared at Peter. Mr. One Thousand and One Ways to Get Into Trouble. He made Jonathan look like a saint.

Halfway up the spiral staircase to her room, Elizabeth turned around. "The Three-Star Detective Agency needs to have a meeting. Now."

The three took their places on the rug in Elizabeth's room. Peter sat hunched over, his shoulders in a meek droop. "I don't try to get in trouble," he said. "My mind . . . it just bubbles. I cannot be stopping the ideas."

"Great," said Elizabeth. "Just like last summer. Every time your mind starts bubbling, we get into trouble. So what do we do now? It would be terrible to tell Hattie and Edna we can't work on the case."

"Listen here, chaps. I know what we must be doing." Peter straightened up and raised his index finger. Elizabeth waited for his pronouncement. "We must now be acting perfect. We must . . . I say, old chap, are you listening?"

Jonathan had discovered a piece of candy in his back pocket. He sat on the rug, carefully licking his chocolate-covered fingers like a cat cleaning its paws. "Yeah. I'm listening. You said I'm supposed to be perfect." He finished his clean-up by wiping his hands on his pants.

After a few minutes' work, they came up with a three-point plan. For Part One, they tidied up the house, swept the sand off all the floors, then put a jar of pink roses on the living room table. For Part Two, which Jonathan called lying low, they stayed outside for most of the afternoon. Peter introduced Part Three. He brought glasses of lemonade to Mr. and Mrs. Pollack on the deck. "You have no worries," he said. "The Three-Star Detectives make dinner tonight."

Peter walked to town for a loaf of French bread from the bakery. Elizabeth made a salad, and Jonathan took care of the main dish.

"Jonathan, what *is* this?" Elizabeth stared at a sloppy meat mixture gurgling in the pot. "If you got this recipe from *The Encyclopedia of the Totally Disgusting*, I'm going to take it outside and bury it."

"It's okay," said Jonathan. "I made up the recipe myself. I was gonna use night crawlers but Mom made me use hamburger instead. So I just have to give it a name. You know, like the stuff we eat at school." He dumped the contents into a large bowl and set it on the table. "Tomatoey Beef Bits El Ranchero," he announced. "With garden vegetables." Mr. Pollack gave it a worried sniff.

"Don't worry, Dad," said Jonathan. "It's just hamburger with lots of ketchup. And canned peas." He spooned a large heap onto everyone's plate.

Dinner was almost as quiet as lunch. And the Tomatoey Beef Bits El Ranchero didn't help. Elizabeth hid a pile of it under a lettuce leaf and took another piece of bread.

After the dishes were done, Peter disappeared into his room and came out carrying three small bottles. He set them in front of Mr. and Mrs. Pollack. "Frightfully sorry, my dear chaps," he said. "I give you all my staining powder, and I behave very perfect now. I am a new Peter." Solemnly, he shook hands with each of them, then sat down to write a note of apology to Mr. Edmond.

Peter's humble behavior finally drew a smile from Mrs. Pollack. "*He was indeed an altered Toad!*" she announced in a storybook voice.

Peter looked up from his letter. "A what?"

"*Altered* means *changed*," said Mrs. Pollack. "It's from *Wind in the Willows*. When Mr. Toad gives up his motor cars and learns to be modest and well-behaved."

"Oh, yes. I have read that book in Germany," said Peter. He rose up from his chair and turned toward his audience. "I am indeed an altered . . . how do you say it?"

"Toad," said Elizabeth.

Mrs. Pollack gathered up the bottles of staining powder. "In that case I hereby declare the purple hand incident officially closed," she said. "But we've decided that you three need a break from your mystery. Tomorrow you stay near the house and don't go into town. You can call Hattie and Edna and let them know."

Elizabeth didn't mind having a quiet day. She needed time to look at the old history book about Stone Harbor. Someone had taken the time to steal three copies of the book, one from Rosewood Cottage and two from the library in Spencer. There could only be one reason – the book must contain a clue to the mystery of the stolen scroll.

The next morning, after the sun had melted the chill, Elizabeth spread a blanket under an oak tree in the backyard. The place was perfect for a good long read. A warm breeze rustled through the hedge, picking up the sweet scent of roses and the song of birds hidden in the trees.

Elizabeth lined up her detective equipment on the blanket – red spiral detective notebook, lucky green pen, and large magnifying glass. Rubbing her hands together like a thief about to crack a safe, she picked up *The History of Stone Harbor*. The tattered paper cover showed a dim painting of the town, with its houses hugging the sea. She peered at the cover through the magnifying glass. She could see all the details now – the sailing ships in the harbor, and even the Jeremiah Coffin Inn. She settled back against the tree and opened the book. The beginning of the story started 10,000 years ago with the first Native Americans coming to Maine.

"Elizabeth, are you coming up for air?" Mrs. Pollack looked down at her daughter. "I've already called you twice for lunch."

"Sorry, Mom. I didn't hear you. I'm trying to finish this book today." She closed the book and stretched her arms. She was barely half done.

Elizabeth peered through the hedge and could see Peter and Jonathan down on the beach. They scrambled back and forth, collecting beach wood and hammering together some kind of fort. After lunch she was tempted to join them, but she stuck to her task. She learned every detail about the history of Stone Harbor. The Indian villages, the coming of the white settlers, the townspeople who fought in the Revolutionary War. She read her way through the 1800's. The theft of the Chinese scroll was mentioned only in one brief paragraph.

At ten o'clock that night Elizabeth crawled into bed. Still three chapters. After a final warning to turn off the light, she leaned into a bright patch of moonlight and kept reading. The living room clock struck eleven as she finally closed the book. She listened for a moment. Jonathan and Peter weren't talking anymore. Even her parents were in bed. Only the sea was still awake, its waves whispering in the darkness.

Elizabeth took off her glasses and rubbed her eyes. She had read every word of the book. She had studied the time line at the end, and glanced at a long list of ships built in Maine. She could have aced a history test on the town of Stone Harbor. But she still hadn't found the clue. Why wasn't she smart enough to see it?

Even her favorite pancakes weren't enough to cheer her up the next morning. "I finished reading the history book," she said. "I don't know. Why would anyone want to keep Hattie and Edna from seeing it? There's just one paragraph about the Chinese scroll and that's it. Nothing more about the mystery."

"We'll figure it out," said Jonathan. "And Mom says we can go see Hattie and Edna after breakfast. We're not being punished anymore."

A half hour later the three knocked on the door of Rosewood Cottage. Daisy gave a few yips, but stopped barking as soon as she saw who it was. She trotted happily behind them into the front room.

Edna poured glasses of lemonade and placed a bowl of plump grapes in the middle of the round table. "I guess we'll have to tone it down a bit," she said. "I suppose you got a good talking-to about the staining powder."

Peter stood up. "No worries. I am a completely altered Toad. I give away all my staining powder."

"Well, that's good," said Hattie. "I met Mr. Edmond in the post office today. He's still kinda haired up."

"Haired up?" asked Elizabeth.

"You know, mad – like a dog that gets his hair up when he's growling. But don't you worry. He'll get over it. We're going to amaze everybody when we find that scroll."

Elizabeth popped a grape into her mouth. *If* we find the scroll, she thought. "I guess we don't have anything to report," she said. "I finished *The History of Stone Harbor*, but I didn't find any clue. Just that one paragraph about the theft."

"Well, us Baker Street Girls did some research yesterday," announced Hattie. "Mrs. Patterson, the librarian, helped us. Oh, she wanted to know all the details. She's very interested in the case, you know."

Elizabeth glanced at Jonathan and Peter. Mrs. Patterson! Somehow her name kept coming up.

"We've been thinking about Mrs. Patterson," said Elizabeth carefully. "That maybe . . . well, what if she's the one who's trying to stop us? I mean, she knew Edna had the letter. And she was right outside just before it was stolen. Edna saw her taking a walk."

"And she acted jolly suspicious at the Harborfest," added Peter. "I watched her. She was interested in our trap. Just before Daisy chased Mr. Edmond's backseat, she walked toward the canvas bag, maybe to take the book."

Edna frowned. "Good gracious. We've known Mildred Patterson for years. She's not the kind of person who would do anything dishonest. No. She's certainly not a suspect."

Hattie struggled over to the table with an enormous book. "Don't you worry about the librarian. She's all right, I tell you. And just take a look at what she helped us find. You tell 'em, Edna."

Edna opened the book. "We wanted some information about the Sung Dynasty," she explained. "That's when the stolen Chinese scroll was painted. So Mildred told us about this lady professor who's spending the summer in Stone Harbor – a professor of Chinese history! Well, we went right over to see the professor, and she lent us this art book. Very interesting!" Edna put on a pair of reading glasses glittering with rhinestones. "First of all, the Sung Dynasty in China was over a thousand years ago. And many artists who painted scrolls worked in the court of the emperor. This book says that some of the scrolls were more than just paintings." She looked up. "Some of the scrolls had a poem written next to the picture. A poem written by an emperor or an empress. Those are the imperial scrolls." She continued slowly, emphasizing each word. "And they are very rare and valuable."

"Wait a minute!" said Elizabeth. "The Chinese scroll we're looking for has writing next to the painting. Chinese characters. It says so in *The History of Stone Harbor*."

"Exactly," said Edna.

"So it might be one of those rare ones," shouted Jonathan.

Hattie jumped up and closed the window. "Not so loud," she said. "We don't want anyone to find out about this."

"I say," said Peter. "This is a bit of all right."

"Course we don't know for sure exactly where to *look* for the scroll," said Hattie.

"And whoever is trying to stop us has a head start finding it," said Edna.

Elizabeth unzipped her backpack and took out her shiny red detective notebook. "Time to review the clues," she announced. "*How to Think Like a Detective.* Chapter six. It says a good detective reviews all the clues on a regular basis. Maybe something important wasn't noticed at first."

Elizabeth opened her notebook. "Okay. This is what we have. We think the mystery man must have been a sailor. And he talked about Stone Harbor and the legend of the ghost ships, so he probably lived here at some time. We know he was in Portland, Maine in 1890, and he was sick with a fever. When he confessed to stealing the scroll, this is what he said. *I'm the one who took it, but no one knows. The scroll is safe. Hidden away. Hidden away and rolled up tight.* He called out for someone named Rebecca. And . . . well, that's about it."

For a moment no one spoke. Three days on the case, and they had no idea who the mystery man was.

Edna took off her reading glasses and stared out the window. "Sunset Point," she muttered. "The children must go to Sunset Point."

Hattie squinted at her friend. "What's going on with you, Edna? You're lookin' awful unrestful. And what's all this about Sunset Point?"

"It's just . . . well, you won't like this, Hattie. You'll say my imagination is running wild again. But I remembered something. I had a dream last night about my grandmother. The one who was accused of stealing the scroll. The two of us were walking down a long road. We came to a woods and then she stopped. We stood right by the sign that says Sunset Point." Edna closed her eyes. "I could even smell the pine trees. Such a strong, sweet fragrance. Grandma pointed into the woods and told me to follow the path." Edna opened her eyes. "And then . . . Well, I guess I woke up. I don't remember any more."

"Dreams!" snorted Hattie. "Next thing, you'll be trying to talk to the mystery man beyond the grave."

Edna rose slowly from her chair and walked over to an old wooden desk under the window. "I don't care what you say, Hattie. That dream was so real. As if . . . as if my grandmother was sending a message. Telling us that something at Sunset Point would help with our mystery."

"Or maybe telling us you had too many raw oysters for dinner," grumbled Hattie. "That always gives you strange dreams. You know it does."

Edna waved away Hattie's comment. "I'd go myself, but the path is too steep." She took a map from the drawer and spread it out on the round table. "Sunset Point is on the west side of the bay." She pointed to a spot on the map.

Jonathan looked down. "But what is Sunset Point?"

"It's a nature preserve," said Edna. "Just about the prettiest spot of land around here. A family named Tuttle used to own it. About ten years ago, old Mrs. Tuttle gave the land to the town. She had one condition – that no houses be built there. It has to stay natural."

Peter stood up. "My dear lady, we must follow your dream. We must go to this Sunset Point." Elizabeth ducked as he flung out his arm and pointed into the distance. "We must go today and follow the ghostly clue!"

"Ghostly clue," grumbled Hattie. "It's more like a bunch of flapdoodle, if you ask me!"

An Unexpected Discovery

"Let me get this straight." Mrs. Pollack stood in the living room of their vacation house. Behind her the wall of windows showed the ocean sparkling with sunlight. "You want to go on a hike. A long one. On a hot day. And you don't care about the mosquitoes."

Three heads nodded in unison. Jonathan took a deep breath. "See, there are these scrolls from China, and they have pictures painted on them. But sometimes they don't just have pictures, they have writing on them too. Not just any old writing. The writing might be a poem that an emperor wrote. Or a lady emperor wrote. She's called an empress. See, this is really cool, because the stolen scroll has Chinese writing on it. And the writing might be one of those royal poems. Then it would be an imperial scroll. And it would be worth lots of money. So Edna had this dream about her grandmother. And she told Edna . . . not the real Edna, but the Edna in the dream . . . that she should walk in the woods at a place called Sunset Point. But the real Edna, not the Edna in the dream, can't walk very far, and . . ."

Mrs. Pollack swatted the air, as if she were warding off a fly. "Don't tell me any more," she said. "We'll go. I'm not sure why, but we'll go."

The group drove off just after lunch, following the route Edna had plotted on the map. Soon they turned off the main highway, winding past a long narrow bay.

"I don't know. We should have been there by now." Mr. Pollack looked up from the map and peered into the distance.

"Edna said there's a sign for Sunset Point just after the woods start," said Elizabeth. As she spoke, they rounded a bend and saw a line of trees ahead.

"Stop the car, Mom. I see it!" Jonathan pointed to a small sign with deeply carved letters. *Sunset Point Nature Preserve.* Mrs. Pollack pulled the car onto a patch of gravel next to the road.

Behind the sign a narrow path led into the woods. Elizabeth was the last one out of the car. She stopped and put on her backpack. This was the very spot where Edna had stood in her dream. The sign. The path. The sun-sweet scent of pine. And the pale hand of her grandmother pointing into the woods.

Elizabeth tugged at the strap on her backpack. She didn't believe in ghostly clues. She was here to please Edna, that was all. How could a walk in the woods help them find a Chinese scroll stolen a hundred years ago? It just wasn't logical. Or scientific.

Mr. Pollack put his arm around her shoulder. "Are the Three-Star Detectives ready to investigate?"

"I guess." Elizabeth looked at her partners. Jonathan pranced around, slicing the air with a stick. Peter was busy decorating himself with equipment – cell phone on his belt, binoculars around his neck, camera in his hand. He looked down at a giant-sized watch. "It is twelve thirty-four and forty seconds," he said. "Tally-ho, chaps. We find the clue now."

Peter plunged into the forest, holding his digital camera in front of his chest. Pine trees, as tall as ship masts, shot up on both sides of the path.

"Peter, we'll never get to Sunset Point if you take so many pictures," said Elizabeth.

Peter raised his index finger. "Technology," he said importantly.

Elizabeth sighed. Words of wisdom were sure to follow.

"This camera," said Peter. "It sees things better than the eye." He turned a full circle. "And there is much mystery here. In Germany we say *Hexenwald*, a witch's woods. With many places to hang their capes." He aimed his camera at a dead pine tree, with a stubble of broken branches.

Elizabeth didn't know about witches, but something *was* different about this place. It was the moss, she decided – spilling everywhere, over rocks and boulders and fallen trees. The forest floor looked soft and round, the way she imagined the bottom of the sea.

"Mosquitoes!" yelled Mrs. Pollack from behind. "We can't keep stopping!"

The group continued, teetering down the rough path in single file. Elizabeth kept her eyes on the tree roots slithering across the trail.

"Hey, Elizabeth, you gotta smell my hands!" Jonathan came at her with his palms up.

"Get away from me!" Elizabeth lurched forward and tripped on a tree root. Jonathan gave her a hand and helped her up. Elizabeth looked down, then glared at Jonathan. Sticky dark patches spotted her hand.

"Pine sap!" he announced. "Now you can smell it on your own hands."

"Lovely." Elizabeth edged past Peter. "Excuse me, old chap. You shall now have the honor of walking in front of my brother."

Elizabeth walked carefully, checking now and then to make sure Jonathan wasn't sneaking up behind her. Finally, she saw a cross-shaped sign ahead and a hint of a path breaking off to the left. *Sunset Point*, it read. Elizabeth could already see a glint of blue through the trees. Ducking under the long arms of a pine tree, she made her way out of the dark woods.

"Wait 'til you see this!" Elizabeth felt as if she had opened a door and walked out into the sky. She found herself high above the ocean, on a shelf of pink rock as big as a room. Far below, a scattering of tiny islands lay like pebbles tossed into the sea.

The others scrambled out of the woods. "I am liking this Sunset Point," said Peter. He scanned the sea with his binoculars. "And maybe I find our clue."

Elizabeth took her turn at the binoculars. The islands zoomed up close, each with a tumble of rocks and a wall of pine trees feathering the sky. Elizabeth wondered how many little islands were off the coast of Maine. Hundreds? Thousands? If the Chinese scroll had been buried on some island, they might as well give up right now.

After sandwiches were passed out, Elizabeth found a spot of shade and sat down with her back against a rock. She opened her backpack and pulled out *The History of Stone Harbor*. The dusty old book with the faded cover was their best chance for finding a clue. Not some haunted forest or island in the sea.

With a sandwich in one hand, she balanced the book in her lap. Elizabeth shot a few darting glances at Jonathan. Only the tips of her fingers were free of pine sap. She turned carefully to page 181. Elizabeth knew the paragraph almost by heart. John Morgridge, a local sea captain, had made a fortune in the China Trade. He presented the scroll to the town in 1850 and had a fancy glass display case built. Forty years later a town hall employee came to work and found the display case smashed open and the scroll gone. Elizabeth tapped her finger on the questions at the bottom of the page. *Who took the Chinese scroll from the town hall on that spring night in 1890? Does the scroll still exist, hidden in some secret place?*

Elizabeth looked up, squinting her eyes at the hazy place where the sea met the sky. They *should* be able to solve this puzzle. They had more clues than in any of their other cases. They knew that a man had confessed to stealing the scroll. He was sick with a fever in 1890. He was probably a sailor who came from Stone Harbor, Maine. He knew someone named Rebecca. And he talked about ghost ships sailing by in the moonlight. But his name. Without knowing the mystery man's name, how would they ever figure out where to look for the scroll?

Mrs. Pollack settled down next to her. "Maybe what you need is a lucky break."

"I don't think so, Mom. I just need to figure things out."

"There's nothing wrong with hoping for a lucky break, you know," said Mr. Pollack. "Even scientists discover things by accident. Penicillin, for example."

"I know about that," said Jonathan. He grinned at his sister. "I read about it in *The Encyclopedia of the Totally Disgusting*. And it's all about mold. Some guy was trying to grow bacteria. But the bacteria wouldn't grow on a spot that got moldy."

"That *guy*, as you put it, was Sir Alexander Fleming," said Mr. Pollack. "And he realized that something in the mold was fighting the bacteria." He turned to Elizabeth. "That's the mark of a good scientist. And a good detective too. They're smart enough to recognize a lucky break when they see one."

Peter had already finished his lunch. He paced restlessly. "We must move on, chaps. Follow the path and find the dream clue."

A few minutes later they slipped back into the dim shadows of the forest and continued along the path. Soon they came to a sunny meadow dotted with daisies. The path narrowed to a thread, winding past scrubby trees and jagged boulders. It ended at another cross-shaped sign. One arm pointed to the right. *Trail*. The other pointed to the left. *Cemetery*. Jonathan and Peter were already heading towards the left.

Three rows of tired gravestones tilted like crooked teeth.

Elizabeth trudged along after the others. She was in no mood for poking around in a cemetery. The path ended at a rough patch of grass marked off by a low wire fence. Inside, three rows of tired gravestones tilted like crooked teeth.

"I'll wait here," said Elizabeth. She stood outside in the shade. The others squeezed through a rusty gate, stuck half open in the tall grass.

Jonathan walked slowly along a row of stones. He stopped in front of one and leaned over. "Hey, Elizabeth, you gotta see this."

Elizabeth took a step back. Whenever Jonathan said she had to see something, it usually meant she should start running in the opposite direction. "That's okay, Jon. I can see from here."

"No, you have to come close. This one's really old. And there's a ship carved on it."

"Oh, all right." Elizabeth went through the gate and stood next to Jonathan. The spotty face of the gravestone was worn almost smooth. The dim outline of a sailing ship could still be seen. Elizabeth pointed to the worn letters. *August 23, 1879. Here lies Josiah Tuttle. Captain of the Ship Isabella.*

All at once, Elizabeth drew back her hand. She flung her backpack on the ground and grabbed *The History of Stone Harbor*. Quickly she turned to the last pages of the book and ran her finger down a long list.

"Jonathan! I could just . . . I could just . . . hug you."

Jonathan shrank back, saucer-eyed, ducking away from his sister's outstretched arms. "No way!" He slipped out the gate and sprinted down the path back to the open field. Elizabeth ran after him. "Rebecca!" she shouted. "Rebecca!"

With the others jogging behind her, she found Jonathan hiding behind a large boulder. "Rebecca! Don't you get it? I figured it out."

"Mom, save me!" Jonathan ran and hid behind Mrs. Pollack. "She's gone weird. She thinks I'm Rebecca."

"I say," called Peter in Elizabeth's direction. "Steady on, old chap!"

A moment later Elizabeth stood panting beside them. "I'm Sir Alexander Fleming! And I just discovered penicillin." She grabbed Mr. and Mrs. Pollack by the hands. "We have to go back to the cemetery. Right now." She pulled them down the path and through the gate to the graveyard. Jonathan and Peter followed at a distance.

Elizabeth pointed to the gravestone with the carved ship. "This is my lucky break!" She whirled around to face the two boys. "What does that gravestone tell you? Jonathan?"

"Uh . . . well . . . it just says that Josiah Tuttle died in 1879."

"But it tells us more than that," said Elizabeth. "The gravestone says Josiah Tuttle was the captain of a ship named *Isabella*. So that means a ship could have a woman's name. Like Isabella or . . ."

"Rebecca!" Jonathan hopped in a circle. "*Rebecca*'s a ship! *Rebecca*'s a ship!"

Elizabeth opened the history book and pointed to the last page. "I just checked the list of ships built in Maine. Listen to this." She read aloud. "*Rebecca. Three-masted schooner, built in Portland, Maine, in 1870. Sank in a storm off the southern coast of Maine in 1888.*"

"So if the Rebecca sank," said Mrs. Pollack, "it would have been a ghost ship. That would explain why the mystery man was talking about looking out to sea in the moonlight. Maybe he was hoping to see the *Rebecca*."

Elizabeth held up the history book. "And it explains why someone wanted to keep this book away from Hattie and Edna. The ship *Rebecca* is listed in here. It's the clue I've been looking for. I know it is."

"Good work, old chap," said Peter. "I would never think of that. When the mystery man called for Rebecca, he called not for a person. But a ship."

Elizabeth looked at her father, who was gazing silently at the gravestone. "I know what you're thinking, Dad. You're going to get all scientific and say there's no proof that Rebecca is a ship."

"I'm not saying you're wrong," said Mr. Pollack. "But we haven't proved it. This is . . . let's see. This is a promising avenue of research. But we have to find out more about the ship called *Rebecca*."

"I know, Dad. I know." But Elizabeth was already celebrating inside. The mystery man had something to do with the ship *Rebecca*. She was sure. Her detective handbook called this a turning point. It was like a flash of lightning cutting through the night. And just for a second, the whole world is bright and clear. The ship called *Rebecca* could lead them to find out who the mystery man was. And then – maybe, just maybe, they would find where the Chinese scroll lay hidden for over a hundred years.

Jonathan stopped hopping. "Wait a minute. The person who took the books. The one who doesn't want us working on the case. That person knows about the clue. And that means . . ."

"Don't say it," said Elizabeth. She knew very well what Jonathan meant. They weren't the only ones looking for the scroll. If they didn't hurry, someone else might find it first!

"Stop!" Peter put his fingers to his lips. "No talking, chaps. Someone comes." They could hear voices nearby. A teenage couple came walking down the path, dressed in shorts and heavy hiking boots. The two stood uncertainly at the cemetery gate. The boy grunted something that sounded like *Hello.*

Peter raised his hand in greeting, then marched out of the cemetery. He and Jonathan rushed down the path toward the car.

Elizabeth hurried after them. "What's going on? Why are you running?"

"I am not liking those chaps," said Peter. "They are. . . How do you say it? They are suspicious characters. Following us to the cemetery. And the girl. She looked at us very strange."

Elizabeth rolled her eyes. "Peter, they didn't follow us to the cemetery. And anyway, I know who they are. You remember Tom, Hattie's nephew. The one who brought her the keys to the inn. That's his son. I saw his picture at Hattie's house. He's probably just taking a walk with his girlfriend."

"Yeah," said Jonathan. "That's why I ran away. They were holding hands." He bent over and made a gagging noise.

A short path through the woods led back to the road where their car was parked. They waited by the car until Mr. and Mrs. Pollack walked out of the woods.

"It's only 2:30, Mom," said Elizabeth. "We still have time to find out about the *Rebecca.*"

Mrs. Pollack pulled the car back onto the dirt road. "Well, when I want to find something, I always start at the library. How about going to the library in Stone Harbor?"

Elizabeth looked at Peter and Jonathan. The Stone Harbor library was the last place they wanted to go. "I don't think the Stone Harbor library is open in the afternoon, Mom. And besides, Mrs. Patterson, the librarian . . . well, she's . . . kind of a suspect."

Mr. Pollack turned around in his seat. "A suspect? What do you mean?"

"We think the librarian might be the one who's trying to stop us from working on the case. She knew Edna had the letter about the mystery man. And she was outside Rosewood Cottage just before the letter and the history book were stolen."

"Jolly suspicious," added Peter.

"And there's one more thing," said Elizabeth. "At the Harborfest, she was . . ." Elizabeth was going to mention Peter's trap, how Mrs. Patterson was walking toward the book just before Mr. Edmond grabbed it. She decided not to bring up anything to remind her parents of the staining powder. "Uh, she was acting suspicious there too."

Mrs. Pollack stopped the car where the gravel road met the highway. "Okay. If the Stone Harbor library isn't open, let's go to Spencer. The library there is bigger, and you won't run into your suspicious Mrs. Patterson."

The town of Spencer was on the far side of the peninsula. The road snaked along, passing overgrown lanes that beckoned with hand-made signs. Misty Shore. Enchanted Forest. Heron Cove. Elizabeth usually liked to close her eyes and let the words turn into pictures in her mind. But not today. Today she felt like a bloodhound straining at the leash. She could think of nothing but the *Rebecca*. And the mystery man.

Finally, near the tip of the peninsula, the road narrowed. A row of generous white mansions guided them into the town of Spencer. Up the hill from the harbor, Mrs. Pollack pulled over on a shady street near the center of town. The group set off across the lawn of the town common, with its crisscross of paths. When they reached the center, Mr. Pollack stopped. "I've read about this town," he said. "If you stand right on this spot and look around, every building you see is at least 150 years old."

Elizabeth gazed at the old buildings, with their white wood softened by afternoon shadows. They were serious buildings, square and simple, with neat rows of shuttered windows.

"Hey! I bet that's the library!" Jonathan took off down the path toward the only stone building. A rounded front marked by smooth white pillars announced its importance. Elizabeth could see letters carved over the wide doorway. *Within These Walls Lies a Treasure of Knowledge.*

Somewhere, she thought, buried in the library's books and papers, was the clue they needed about the ship *Rebecca*.

Elizabeth followed the others through a set of heavy doors. The main room was round, with walls that soared up to a high dome. They creaked across a shiny wooden floor sprinkled with patches of sunlight.

"*Ja, endlich!*[5]" Peter ran over to a table where two computers sat side by side. Elizabeth wouldn't have been surprised if he had put his arms around them. He hurried over to the circulation desk. "I may use it, yes?" He signed his name on a list, then slid into a chair in front of the screen. The others stood in a circle behind him.

Elizabeth could see Peter puffing himself up, like a bird getting ready to preen.

---

[5] *Ja, entlich* (Yah, ENT-lish). Yes, finally.

"I know, Peter. Technology is the future of crime detection. And you're going to solve the whole mystery on the computer."

"Exactly, old chap. You just tell me again about the *Rebecca*. What kind of ship."

"A three-masted schooner," said Elizabeth. She spelled the last word for him.

Peter began clicking the mouse until he came up with a search box on the screen. "*Rebecca Maine three-masted schooner*," he typed.

Within seconds the sites rolled down the page. They were able to discover when and where the *Rebecca* was built. How many tons of cargo she held. Where she was headed the day she sank.

"This will help," said Peter. "It says *Rebecca* was carrying a cargo of lumber and sank on September 18, 1888. We have now the right date."

Another fifteen minutes didn't bring any new information. "But we still don't know enough," said Elizabeth. "We have to know more about what happened when the *Rebecca* sank."

"If I were you," said Mrs. Pollack, "I'd ask the reference librarian. She might have some ideas."

Elizabeth spotted the reference desk at the far end of the next room. The others followed as she walked up to the counter. A woman stood behind the desk, leaning over a book. She looked up and smiled. "Can I help you?"

"Oh!" Elizabeth's mouth fell open like a loose flap. Impossible! The woman looking down at her was their number one suspect – Mrs. Patterson, the Stone Harbor librarian.

Mrs. Patterson's smile widened. "Why, I know you!" she said. "You're the ones helping Hattie and Edna with their mystery." She leaned forward eagerly. "Are you working on your mystery right now? Can I do something for you?"

Elizabeth felt Jonathan's knuckle boring into her back. She didn't need to be reminded not to give away their clue.

"Well, uh . . . we just . . . didn't know you worked here."

"I work here a few afternoons a week." Mrs. Patterson looked at the whole group. "Do you need help with something?"

Jonathan lunged forward. "Warts!" The word burst out like a blast from a tuba. "You can help me with warts!"

Mrs. Patterson's smile faded.

"I mean, I don't have any warts," said Jonathan, "but lots of people do. Some people get boils too. And carbuncles, and scabs, and blisters and things like that. Even something called a bleb, but you probably never heard of it. That's a kind of blister with blood in it. I read about all that stuff in my . . . in my scientific encyclopedia. Uh, . . . so it's good to know about them."

Mrs. Patterson's chin disappeared into her neck as she slowly leaned away from Jonathan.

Elizabeth gave her brother a nudge. "Quit babbling. And get to the point."

"So anyway, I was thinking maybe you could help me find out about warts. Because . . . because that's what I'm gonna do for my science fair project. Someday."

"Well," said Mrs. Patterson uncertainly. "I suppose I could help you find some information. Just follow me, please." As Jonathan trotted after Mrs. Patterson, he gave the others a thumbs-up sign behind his back. "And I'm looking for volume two of a certain book," he added. "It's called *The Encyclopedia of the Totally Disgusting*."

"By Jove!" whispered Peter. "This boy is a genius. He will keep our suspect very busy."

"Suspect?" whispered Mr. Pollack.

Elizabeth realized that her parents hadn't recognized the Stone Harbor librarian. "Don't worry. I'll explain in a minute."

A slender young woman walked up behind them. "Can I help you find anything?"

Elizabeth glanced over her shoulder and saw that Mrs. Patterson and Jonathan were at the far end of the room. "Uh, yes." Elizabeth spoke slowly, careful not to give too much information. "We'd like to find out about a shipwreck. It happened a long time ago. In 1888. Off the coast of southern Maine."

"Let's see. We've got some books on shipwrecks, but I'm not sure the one you want would be covered, unless it's a very famous one."

"No, I don't think it's famous," said Elizabeth.

"Then the best way would be to look at an old newspaper. If you know the exact date, I could show you how to find it. Our local newspaper probably covered the story."

"Permit me, my good lady," said Peter. He handed her a piece of paper. "I give you the exact date. I have found it in the computer."

"Good. That's just what I need." The young woman led them past Jonathan and Mrs. Patterson, who were standing in front of a computer screen.

"I don't see anything listed under *warts*," Mrs. Patterson was saying. "Let's try skin diseases." To Elizabeth's relief, the newspapers were around the corner, well away from Mrs. Patterson.

The librarian opened a narrow metal drawer. "Here they are," she said. "*The Spencer Daily Journal*. They go back to 1858. What date did you say you wanted?"

"September, 1888." Elizabeth had expected a pile of brittle old newspapers. Instead the drawer contained rows of small white boxes.

"You want the newspapers for the last six months of 1888," said the librarian. "Here it is." She lifted out one of the boxes. "It's all on microfilm. You see, each page gets photographed. To look at the pages, you just run the film through a machine." The librarian brought them to a machine with a large, square screen. After showing them how to use it, she walked back to the reference desk.

Elizabeth sat in front of the machine and looked up at her parents. "You're probably wondering about the warts," she said. "You're not going to believe this, but the reference librarian is Mrs. Patterson. Our suspect. I guess she works here in the afternoon when the Stone Harbor library is closed."

Mrs. Pollack smiled. "Now I get it. Jonathan is keeping Mrs. Patterson busy with warts while we look for our clue."

Peter walked to the end of the newspaper aisle and peered around the corner. "I will keep watch," he whispered.

"Good idea. I'll try and get this done fast." Elizabeth turned a knob at the bottom of the machine. Images of newspaper pages flew across the screen. She stopped. The newspaper page was dated July 3, 1888. She stopped again. August 15. She turned the knob again, slowly this time. The pages rolling across the screen were dated in September.

"Here it is," cried Elizabeth. "September 18, 1888." Mr. and Mrs. Pollack leaned over and scanned each page together with Elizabeth. They learned that a man had shot his uncle, thinking he was a burglar. A worker broke his leg falling into a hole. The government passed a new tax. Not a word about a shipwreck.

"Wait a minute! We're looking at the wrong day!" said Mr. Pollack. "The shipwreck wouldn't be in the newspaper the same day it happened. It wouldn't have been reported until the next day!"

Elizabeth began rolling the pages across the screen. They didn't have much time.

"Oh, dash it all," whispered Peter. "Mrs. Patterson. She comes this way! I must get her away!" Peter stepped out from the shelf and nearly collided with their suspect. "My dear lady," he said. "I am needing help. Much help. I need information about . . . about . . ." Elizabeth held her breath. She hoped Peter would be able to think of something other than warts. "About warthogs," boomed Peter. "Warthogs. They are a problem in Germany, you know, where I come from." Peter and Mrs. Patterson walked away toward the reference desk. They could hear Mrs. Patterson's voice. "That's odd. I thought warthogs were native to Africa."

Elizabeth went back to work. The front page from September 19 rolled slowly across the screen. A three-word headline screamed across the page. *Disaster at Sea!*

Elizabeth leaned toward the screen. She could feel the words pulling her back into the past, to a place where long-forgotten secrets were hidden. She whispered the first paragraph aloud. *The three-masted schooner Rebecca met a tragic fate during Wednesday's destructive wind storm. Bound for Cuba with a cargo of lumber, the ship lost a mast and was driven into the rocks off Thompson Island. High seas prevented any attempt at rescue. All crew members were killed but one."* Elizabeth stopped. She tried to slow down her thoughts, but the ideas were flashing, exploding like fireworks. One person survived the sinking of the *Rebecca*. One person. What if . . . ? What if that one survivor was the mystery man?

"Keep reading," whispered Mr. Pollack. "We think the mystery man came from Stone Harbor. Let's see if the article says where the survivor was from."

Elizabeth read the last two sentences in a shaky voice. *"The surviving crew member was found clinging to a piece of wreckage the next morning. He is Benjamin Thomas of . . . ,"* Elizabeth looked up at her father, *"of Stone Harbor, Maine."*

Mr. Pollack put his hand on Elizabeth's shoulder. "If I had to give an unscientific guess," he said. "I'd say you just found your mystery man."

A New Surprise

Elizabeth gripped the arms of her chair. She felt like dancing with joy, but she didn't dare give herself away.

Mrs. Pollack fished a coin out of her purse. "Dad and I will make a photocopy of this page and rewind the film," she said quickly. "You go round up Peter and Jonathan."

Elizabeth spotted Jonathan in the main reading room. He was grinning down at a thick book open on the table.

"You gotta see this, Elizabeth. It's called *Diseases of the Skin*. There's all kinds of stuff I didn't even know about. And look at all these pictures. Close-ups!" He shoved a book under her nose. The picture, showing something red and swollen, practically oozed off the page.

Elizabeth swatted the book away. "Jonathan, forget about skin diseases. We have to go." She glanced at Mrs. Patterson and Peter on the other side of the room. Elizabeth lowered her voice. "We found something."

"Found what?" asked Jonathan.

"Be quiet. I'll tell you later." Elizabeth dragged him away from his book. "Mom and Dad are already waiting for us by the door."

"But I wanted to check out one of those books. I really might do a science project on warts, you know." Elizabeth kept a firm grip on his arm. On her way out she motioned to Peter. He took leave of Mrs. Patterson with a deep bow. "Thank you, my dear lady. I learn many good things about warthogs."

As soon as Elizabeth got out the door, she turned two cartwheels on the grass then sprinted across the town green with both hands in the air. Jonathan and Peter hurried after her.

"I say, chap!" called Peter. "What did you find?" He and Jonathan caught up with Elizabeth as they reached the car. Elizabeth hopped into the backseat.

"The mystery man," she panted. "I think I know who he is." She told them about the newspaper describing the sinking of the *Rebecca* and the lone survivor, Benjamin Thomas.

"Now you've got a lead that can be checked," said Mr. Pollack. "You can find out more about Benjamin Thomas."

"And then," said Peter grandly, "we know all about the thief. And we find the Chinese scroll."

As soon as they reached their vacation house, Elizabeth phoned Rosewood Cottage.

"I talked to Hattie," she said as she hung up. "Edna wasn't there. She's at the fix-it shop. That's what Hattie calls it when Edna gets her hair done. Then they're going to play bingo at the Senior Center."

"So did you tell her?" asked Jonathan.

"I just told her we found out something big. And we'll tell them tomorrow when we have our case meeting."

The next morning, at exactly ten o'clock, the three detectives stood at the door of Rosewood Cottage. "Don't turn around," whispered Elizabeth. "And don't move. Mr. Edmond's coming. And he's still got purple hands." The three stood at the door, stiff as fence posts. Mr. Edmond glared at them before walking into the library. "Juvenile delinquents," he snarled. "That's what you are."

Elizabeth's quick tap on the door was answered with Hattie's voice. "Come on in. It's open. Just make sure Daisy stays put." The three squeezed through the door, then closed it quickly. Daisy, with a red bandana around her neck, raced from one to the other, demanding attention. Peter was the first to enter the front room.

"I say, ladies! Good show!"

Rosewood Cottage was decked out for a party. On the round table, delicate china cups and saucers surrounded a golden brown coffee cake. Edna sat at the table in a bright flowered dress. Her snow white hair was newly puffed. "I baked a Swedish tea ring," she said. "Hattie told me you've had a breakthrough. Sounded like a good excuse for a celebration." Hattie squirmed and tugged at her lavender dress, but gave a bright pink smile. She was wearing lipstick.

After everyone took their places around the table, Edna passed Elizabeth a cup of tea and a plate of cake. "Now that we're all together," she said. "We can't wait to hear the news."

Elizabeth opened her mouth to speak. Too late. "We have followed Edna's dream," sputtered Peter. A few cake crumbs flew out, which Daisy rounded up immediately. "We have gone to Sunset Point. We have had adventures at the library. We . . . ," he swallowed and continued in a loud voice. "We figured out who the mystery man is."

"That's just what I was hoping you would say," said Edna. "Clearing my grandmother's name means so much to me." She clasped her hands together with an eager smile. The three detectives filled in all the details, starting with the cemetery at Sunset Point and ending with the newspaper article about the *Rebecca*.

"A buryin' ground!" said Hattie. "Fancy that! Finding a clue on a gravestone." She took a sip of tea. "Now I'm burstin' to know. What's the name of the man who survived the shipwreck? The one you think confessed to stealing the scroll."

Elizabeth opened her notebook. "He came from Stone Harbor," she said. "And his name was. . ." She glanced down at the page. "His name was Benjamin Thomas."

Hattie's smile vanished. She clattered her tea cup down on the table as she jumped up from her chair. "It can't be!" She turned away, leaning on the mantel. Edna got up and put her hand on Hattie's shoulder. "I'm sorry, Hattie. I never thought it would turn out like this."

"I say," said Peter. "This news. It is bad?"

Edna turned toward them. "It's just the shock," she said. "You see, Benjamin Thomas is . . . Hattie's grandfather."

Hattie's grandfather? Elizabeth's happy mood wilted. They wanted to prove Edna's grandmother innocent. And now it looked like Hattie's grandfather was the one who confessed to the crime. "I'm sorry. Hattie, are you all right?"

"I'll be fine. This just takes some gettin' used to." Hattie's voice had gone flat. "Excuse me, please. I think I better call my nephew Tom."

No one spoke a word while Hattie was gone. Only Daisy was happy. She had snatched Peter's fork and sat hunched under the table licking it clean.

Hattie came back into the room a few minutes later. She sat down at the table with her hands folded in her lap. "I forgot. Tom's still out of town," she said. "He won't be back for a few days."

Elizabeth didn't like seeing Hattie so meek – like a boat with no wind in its sails.

"Maybe it's all wrong," said Jonathan. "Maybe Benjamin Thomas isn't really the mystery man."

Elizabeth looked down at her notebook. As the others listened, she read her notes aloud. "The man who confessed to the theft talked about Stone Harbor. When he was sick with a fever, he kept calling out the name *Rebecca* and talking about a legend of sunken ships. Everything fits with Benjamin Thomas. He was from Stone Harbor, and he sailed on a ship called *Rebecca*. He was the only person to survive when it sank."

"Do you think your grandfather was ever in Portland?" asked Edna. "Because we know the mystery man was in the hospital there in 1890."

Hattie spoke softly. "My grandfather was a sailor. But he didn't sail on ships from Stone Harbor. My grandmother told me he used to always leave from . . . from Portland." Hattie rubbed her forehead. "I know it shouldn't bother me so much. But the past just seems very close to us here. The same families have been in Stone Harbor for hundreds of years."

"Can you tell us anything else about your grandfather?" asked Elizabeth softly.

"Not much. I never met him. He died when my father was a baby, probably around 1893. All I know is that my Grandfather Benjamin went on long voyages and sent money home. He got sick on one of his trips and died somewhere in Asia." She walked over to the mantel and picked up a tiny sleigh carved out of wood. She held it out in her palm. "This little toy is all I have from him. He made it for my father." Hattie slumped back into her chair. "My grandfather a thief. I just can't fathom it."

Elizabeth stared at the floor, waiting for someone else to say something. For once she was glad to see Peter puff himself up. "See here, chaps. I am knowing no reason to be gloomy. Now we know the mystery man. This will help us. We now will find the Chinese scroll."

Hattie wiped her eyes, then honked a few times into her handkerchief. "You're right," she said. "No use snivellin'. Doesn't do a bit of good. We need to find out more about my grandfather, that's for sure. If he was the thief, it's all the more reason to set things right." She leaned forward. "And another thing. Don't tell *a soul* about this. Except your parents, of course. You can tell them, but no one else." She looked over her shoulder, as if someone might be listening. "We still don't know who's trying to scare us off this case."

Scare us off the case. Elizabeth felt a hot rush of fear. She didn't like to think about the person who had followed them into the Jeremiah Coffin Inn. And who sneaked into Rosewood Cottage to steal the old letter and the history book. And who must be looking for the Chinese scroll.

Elizabeth felt Edna's soft hand patting her on the shoulder. "Don't worry, dear. I know it seems like someone has a head start on us, but when the Baker Street Girls and the Three-Star Detectives put their heads together, they can outsmart anyone." Edna cut more pieces of coffee cake. "I'm wondering about one thing, Hattie. What about your grandmother? Do you think she knew anything about the theft?"

"My Grandma Josephine? Well, if she did know, she never told anyone else in the family. Unless . . ."

Hattie turned away from the others and settled into a rocking chair in the corner. "Don't mind me. I just have to sit here and have myself a little think." Elizabeth could hear her muttering something about her grandmother. Hattie rocked slowly, leaning her head against the high wooden back. "I used to visit my grandmother. But it was so long ago." Hattie closed her eyes. "If I could just remember . . ."

Suddenly Hattie sprang up. "Eat up, friends. We still have time if we light out quick."

"Time for what?" asked Edna.

"I'm going to take the children on the mail boat to Turtle Island," said Hattie. "It leaves from Stone Harbor at 11:30."

Elizabeth put the cake back down on her plate. "But what's on Turtle Island?"

"The next stop on our trail of clues, that's what." Hattie stood with her hands on her hips. Elizabeth half expected her to fly out the window like Peter Pan. "It's something I haven't seen since I was five or six years old – Grandma Josephine's Mystery Rug!"

In an instant, Elizabeth felt her fears being swept away. She had no idea what Hattie meant, but one thing she knew for sure. Their treasure hunt was about to begin!

The Mystery Rug

Hattie refused to answer any questions. She would only say that her grandmother had made a rug. A rug that might help them with their mystery.

"I'll be back in two shakes. I need to get rid of this dress and get some real clothes on." Hattie hurried out of the room. "And I want to dig out some of my grandmother's letters," she called. "Who knows? There might be a clue."

Elizabeth stepped out into the hallway to use the phone. A few minutes later she hung up with a groan. "Mom says we have to come home and get jackets first. And put on sunscreen. But Dad says he'll bring the stuff and meet us on the beach." Elizabeth wondered what it would be like to be a grown-up detective. Sherlock Holmes was lucky. *He* never had to go home and get a jacket before investigating a case.

Mr. Pollack met them halfway down the beach. He handed over the jackets and sunscreen. "Be careful," he called as they hurried away. "And mind what Hattie tells you."

The three reached the harbor just as the blare of a horn announced the mail boat. Hattie stood on the dock wearing her rolled-up blue jeans and an oversized red sweatshirt. Only the map of wrinkles on her face gave away her age. She held up a handful of tickets. "Come on! You're just in time!"

The three clattered down a wide pier and followed Hattie into the back of a sleek white boat. They made their way past a clutter of boxes filled with groceries. An open doorway led to a covered area with rows of benches.

"Let's go up top," said Hattie. "In the open. If you stay cooped up down here you might as well be ridin' a bus." She took Peter's arm. "I just need some help getting these old legs up the stairs."

At the top they settled onto a metal bench near the front of the boat. Elizabeth sat closest to the rail, with Hattie next to her. She could feel the dull throb of the motor as the boat backed away from the pier. Jonathan and Peter sat at the end of the bench, deep in conversation. Elizabeth didn't know what they were talking about, but she thought she heard the words *candied crickets*.

"You'll be glad you have your jacket," said Hattie. "It's breezin' up good today. East wind blowin' off the sea. My father used to say when you're out on the water you can always feel ice in the wind. Even on the warmest day. That's so you never forget how deep and cold the ocean is."

Elizabeth faced into the wind and closed her eyes. Now she could feel it too – a hint of coolness running like a shiver through the warm breeze. Elizabeth thought about Hattie's grandfather, sailing out on the wide-open sea. She opened her eyes and zipped up her jacket.

"I was just wondering, Hattie," said Elizabeth. "How come the rug is called a mystery rug? Can't you just give a hint?"

"Well, I can tell you this. It's a mystery rug because there's a *secret message* in it."

"A secret message?"

"That's what my grandmother told me. I was so young at the time. My mind gets all fogged up just trying to think about it. But now we're going to the island where Grandma used to live. There's a fair chance the rug is still in the house. Maybe it has something to do with our mystery. And maybe it doesn't. I just figure it's about time someone found out what the secret is." Hattie crossed her arms and leaned back. "We'll stop at two small islands, then Turtle Island is the third. We can't miss it."

"But . . . how can there be a secret message in a rug? I mean . . ." Elizabeth didn't bother finishing her question.

Hattie had nestled her chin onto her chest. She gave a long sigh, then settled into a snore.

The mail boat stopped at two small islands, with rambling houses peeking out from the pine trees. One by one the passengers collected their boxes of groceries and left. The boat continued toward the open sea now, cutting the dark water into fans of white foam.

"Hey, Elizabeth. You better wake up Hattie," called Jonathan. "She said we were the third stop."

As the boat swung around, Elizabeth sat up straight. They were headed for the last harbor island. This one had a lighthouse rising up from the rocks, so white and gleaming it seemed to be pasted onto the blue sky.

"Hattie! Your grandmother lived on a lighthouse island!"

Hattie woke up with a snort. "What? Are we there?"

"Your grandmother," repeated Elizabeth. "She lived on the island with the lighthouse!"

"That's right," said Hattie. She stretched up her arms. "A few years after my grandfather died, Grandma Josephine married again. John Sutherland, a lighthouse keeper. I used to visit them on the island when I was a little tyke. Of course, the beacon light is all automatic now, so no one lives there anymore. But they're making the island into a museum. Fixing up the house just like it used to be in the old days."

A few minutes later a young man waiting on the pier caught the rope and tied up the boat.

Jonathan squeezed past his sister as they stepped off. "Hey, Elizabeth. I like your hair. It looks like a squirrel's nest!" He raced up a steep ramp onto the rocky slope of the island.

"And yours looks like someone combed it with a vacuum cleaner!" Elizabeth smoothed down her wind-whipped hair. What was left of her pony tail hung as limp as a rag.

Hattie spoke for a moment to the young man, then motioned for the others to follow. "He said the museum director, Miss Mason, is up at the house. If anyone knows where the mystery rug is, it'll be her."

A steep path led through a forest of pine trees. "I used to scramble up this trail as spry as a monkey," said Hattie. "But not anymore."

After a few rests they reached the flat top of the island. The path opened onto a wide lawn where patches of bare rock poked up through the grass. Straight ahead was the thick base of the lighthouse, with a tidy white house huddled next to it.

Hattie stopped at the edge of the woods. "Now, just stop for a minute and smell this air. My grandmother used to say it was like a recipe. One part sea breeze. One part sweet pine. And all mixed in with the heat of the sun. If you ask me, this is just about the handsomest place in the world."

Elizabeth had to agree. It was like a beautiful painting with just three colors: pine green, sky blue, and the clean white of the buildings. Except this was a painting she could step right into, a painting full of sunshine and the far-off cries of sea gulls.

Hattie led the way to the house. She waved to a dark-haired young woman kneeling in a flower bed. The woman shook the dirt off her hands as she stood up.

"Hattie! This is a surprise. I'm always glad to see you though." She pointed to the freshly painted house. "Our grand opening is in two weeks. What do you think?"

"Tip-top shape," said Hattie.

Miss Mason turned to the children. "Hattie's a big part of this project. Her memories are giving us some of our best stories." She went on to tell how they were fixing up the house to look just like it did in 1930.

Elizabeth tried to listen but her mind was back on the mystery. She couldn't wait to find out about the rug. Instead,

Hattie smiled softly. "I don't know what comes over me when I'm back on the island. Seems like the years fold back in on themselves, and I get to feeling like a girl again." She climbed the stairs onto the front porch. "I used to stand at this very spot and look down at the sea. It seemed like I was so high up. Like looking at the world from the sky."

Elizabeth looked at Peter and Jonathan. What about the mystery rug?

Peter stepped forward, whipping a card out of his back pocket. He handed it to Miss Mason. "My good lady. I am Peter Hoffmann, Super Sleuth Extraordinaire."

She answered with a puzzled "Oh, I see."

Hattie finally snapped back to business. "Sorry. I'm gettin' so dreamy and sicky sweet I don't even recognize myself." She stepped off the porch. "First of all, I want you to meet Elizabeth, Jonathan, and Peter. They're all detectives. And smart too. Sharp as a tack."

"We're looking for treasure," said Jonathan.

Elizabeth shook her head at Jonathan. She didn't want him to start blabbing about the mystery.

"I like the sound of that," said Miss Mason. "But how can I help you?"

"One time when I was visiting here," said Hattie, "my Grandma Josephine showed me something special. A little rug she had made. With pictures on it, I think. She kept the rug wrapped up in a sheet to protect it. She told me there was a secret message in the pictures. A message she never figured out." Hattie frowned. "I don't know what became of the rug. I'm thinking it might still be here."

"A small rug." Miss Mason shook her head. "I'm sorry, Hattie. We didn't find any rugs in the house at all. Just some old carpeting we had to tear out."

"But there must be some way we can find it," said Elizabeth.

"I don't know about *finding* the rug, but there might be a way we can see it." Miss Mason walked over to a side door. "Come on in the house. I may have something interesting to show you." She opened the door. "Welcome to the year 1930. And a house without electricity."

They stepped into a sunny kitchen, with flowered curtains riding the breeze from an open window. The room was simple and neat, gleaming under a coat of white paint.

"Nothin' like the slap of a screen door to bring back the old days," said Hattie. "I don't know how you did it, Marsha, but this kitchen is just the way I remember. The hand pump by the sink. And that big old black iron stove." She rubbed her eyes then blinked hard a few times. "I half expect Grandma Josephine to walk in here and bake us a loaf of bread."

Elizabeth looked up at an old wooden clock on a shelf above the kitchen table. She followed the swinging pendulum with her eyes. She had a strange feeling, as if the slow and steady ticking were pushing time backward instead of forward. Elizabeth smiled. The Three-Star detectives were looking for a scroll that was stolen over a hundred years ago. If this house took her back into the past, it was just the place she wanted to be.

"This is capital," said Peter. "*Sehr gut.*[6]" He stood in the middle of the room with his digital camera. Turning a slow circle, he took pictures of every object in the room.

Miss Mason had already walked out of the kitchen. "Just come through here into the dining room," she called. "I'll be back in a minute."

Elizabeth followed the others. The dining room was as cozy as a page out of a picture book. Sunshine warmed the honey-colored floor. The red bricks of the fireplace glowed

---

[6] *Sehr gut* (zehr goot). Very good.

against buttery yellow walls. On a round table, a board game was set up, ready to play.

"Oh, I say."

"I know," said Elizabeth. "This is capital."

"Right-o." Peter stood in front of the mantel, taking pictures of a delicate oil lamp and a model sailing ship.

Miss Mason returned holding a small box. She put down a stack of photos on the table.

"How come you have all these?" asked Jonathan.

"Because pictures come in handy when you're a history detective," said Miss Mason. "You see, we wanted to make the house look the way it did in 1930. But everything had changed. How could we know what it used to look like? I had to look at a lot of old pictures and letters, interview people like Hattie who lived here or visited here. Then we had to track things down. We found the old stove and the pump underneath a pile of wood in the boathouse. We tracked down the kitchen clock at an antique shop. It was like putting a puzzle together."

"Or solving a mystery," said Elizabeth.

"You're right," said Miss Mason. "That's what I love about this job." She looked through the pictures and held up a small black and white photo. "Here's the one I want." She handed Hattie a large round magnifying glass. "This was taken about ten years after your grandmother died. But take a look at what's in front of the fireplace."

Hattie bent over the photo. "That's it," she cried. "Grandma Josephine's mystery rug! It must have been left in the house after she died."

The others crowded around the table. Hattie handed the magnifying glass to Elizabeth. She looked through the glass at the photo. A pouty little girl with long dark hair stood by the fireplace. And next to her . . .

Elizabeth moved the glass back and forth until the picture swelled up big. Next to the girl was . . . the strangest looking rug Elizabeth had ever seen.

The Secret Message

"I can see pictures," said Elizabeth. "And . . . Jonathan, quit breathing on me!" She leaned away from her brother. "I see seven pictures in the top row and seven in the bottom row. It looks like . . . Jonathan, get away from me! Oh, here. You and Peter take a look."

After Jonathan and Peter had taken their turns, Elizabeth looked through the magnifying glass again. She drew a picture of the rug in her detective notebook.

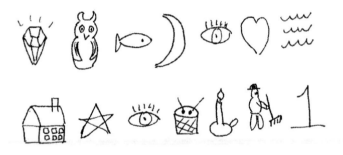

She pointed to the first picture, hoping Jonathan wouldn't snicker at her rough drawings. "That looks like a diamond. Then there's an owl. Fish. Moon. Eye. Heart. Waves. A big house, or maybe an inn. Star. Eye. Drum. Candle. A farmer, I guess. And the number one."

Jonathan looked down at the photo. "Weird."

Miss Mason took another look. "This looks to me like a hooked rug. They were very popular in New England in the old days. Women would use little scraps of material to make the loops. But this . . ." She held the magnifying glass close to the photo. "I've never seen any pattern like this before. I have no idea what it could mean."

"And I'm no help either," said Hattie. "All I remember is that Grandma Josephine said there was a secret message in the pictures. Course if it was easy to figure out, it wouldn't be a *secret* message. Like my father used to say, we've got some ruminatin' to do."

Miss Mason put the photo back into the box. "I'm sorry I can't give you the photograph. But Elizabeth did a good job drawing. You've got the pictures. That's the main thing."

Miss Mason looked at her watch. "I'm forgetting about the time. If you want to catch the next mail boat, we can just make it." They hurried down the stairs and out the back door. Miss Mason took them down a short path through the woods. Soon the pine trees gave way to a jumble of boulders at the edge of the island. The mail boat glided in toward the pier.

"Let's sit below this time," said Hattie. "I've climbed enough stairs for one day." Miss Mason helped her into the boat, then waved as they pulled away from the island.

Elizabeth peeked into her notebook and took one more look at the pictures. They had solved old puzzles from the past before, but now she had no idea where to start. Diamond. Owl. Fish. Moon. What could it mean? And did it have anything to do with their mystery?

"I say, chaps, I think she tries to tell us something," said Peter. Miss Mason stood on the shore with her hands cupped to her mouth. Elizabeth and Peter stuck their heads out the window. All Elizabeth could hear was the drone of the motor and the splash of waves against the boat. "I can't hear what she's saying."

"I hear perfect," said Peter as he sat down. "She says a word again and again. A word I cannot understand. She says *ree-bus*. It maybe has something to do with the rug."

"I don't think so," said Elizabeth. "That doesn't mean anything."

"But it does," said Hattie. "There *is* a word *rebus*. It's some kind of puzzle. I can't remember exactly, but we'll ask Edna. She's good with words."

Hattie was the first one off the boat when they arrived at Stone Harbor. Back at Rosewood Cottage she stomped into the hallway. "Get up from your beauty rest, Edna. The detectives are back!" Daisy yapped and ran around their legs.

"I was *not* taking a nap." Edna's voice came from the front room. "I've been doing some investigating." They walked in and found Edna sitting on the couch amid a sea of papers. "I've been reading through these family letters you brought out, Hattie. I found some from your grandmother. And I did find something interesting." Edna took off her reading glasses. "But first, tell me what happened with the rug."

"We didn't find the rug," said Hattie. "But we found the next best thing – a photograph of it. We couldn't take the photo with us, but Elizabeth drew a real nice picture."

"And we need to know what a word means," said Jonathan. "Ree . . . What is it?"

"Rebus," said Peter. "If I just had my computer."

"You don't need a computer," laughed Edna. "I can tell you what a rebus is. Hattie, don't you remember when we used to write picture letters to each other?" Edna lifted herself off the sofa and walked over to the writing desk. "A rebus uses pictures to take the place of words or syllables. So instead of writing the word *be*, you draw a picture of a bee. The letter *m* plus a picture of an oar would be the word *more*. Here, I'll write one for you." She drew on a piece of paper, then set it down on the round table in front of the others.

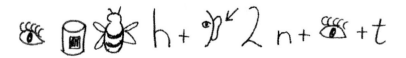

Peter looked down. "This is easy. I can read it perfect." He grabbed the paper. "*I . . . can . . . be . . . here . . . to . . . n . . . ight. I can be here tonight.*"

"Peter the Great," muttered Elizabeth.

"So Miss Mason must have been telling us that the pictures in the rug are a rebus," said Hattie.

"Let me look at your pictures, Elizabeth." Edna studied the notebook. "I can see why she thinks these pictures are a rebus. Look at this. An eye appears twice."

"That's for the word *I*," said Jonathan.

"Right. Or for a syllable that sounds like *I*. It's a common rebus picture."

"I'm wondering, chaps, if this . . . this rebus is about our mystery," said Peter.

Edna stood in the middle of the room leaning on her cane. "It's about our mystery, all right. In fact, I believe this rebus may be the *answer* to our mystery."

Hattie narrowed her eyes. "Edna, have you been eatin' oysters again? You know they make you a little strange."

"No, I have not been eating oysters. You brought out a box of letters before you left for the mail boat. It had some letters from your grandmother." Edna picked up a folded sheet of paper from the table. "It's all right here in a letter to her sister. She wrote about gathering together your grandfather's things after he died. She said she found a folded piece of paper that said *This is where to find it.* When she opened the paper, she saw a strange picture message. That's what she called it. A picture message. She said the first picture was a diamond or some kind of jewel. She didn't understand what it meant or what she was supposed to be looking for."

"And all these years I never read that letter," said Hattie. "Course there are so many. I never looked at each and every one."

"So . . ." Elizabeth looked down at the pictures in her notebook. "Hattie's grandfather drew a rebus. And her grandmother didn't know what it meant. But she made a rug and put the rebus pictures in the pattern. And that means . . . the secret message in the rug is from Benjamin Thomas!"

"I think it is," said Edna. "Just as if he were standing right here talking to us. Telling us where to find the stolen Chinese scroll."

"First order of business," said Hattie. "Let's each make a copy of what Elizabeth drew." She handed out four sheets of paper. "Then we'll all work alone for a little while before we put our heads together and see what we came up with."

With their drawings in hand, Edna and Hattie cleared the letters off the sofa. They sat at opposite ends, with Daisy snoozing in the middle. Jonathan and Peter took the two high-backed chairs. Elizabeth sat at the desk by the window, staring at the pictures. She tried saying the words quickly, but no matter how she put them together, they didn't seem to mean anything. Diamond, owl, fish, moon, eye. She peered at the others. No one had written a word.

After fifteen minutes they gave up and gathered at the round table. "I'm as stuck as a fly in molasses," said Hattie. "I can't figure out a thing."

Elizabeth looked at the others. Even Peter the Great was silent.

"I think I figured out the last two words," said Edna. "That picture of the person with the rake in his hand. I think that's supposed to be *till*. Like tilling the soil. So the last two words would be *till one*. Of course, that doesn't get us very far."

"I think I know where we could get some help," said Elizabeth, "but we'll have to go home first."

Hattie yawned. "Let's check in again after dinner." She shuffled over to the rocking chair. "Actually, I could use a little beauty rest myself."

When Elizabeth and the boys raced into the kitchen of their vacation house, they found Mr. and Mrs. Pollack putting away groceries. After a three-way story of the discoveries at Turtle Island, Mrs. Pollack looked at a bunch of bananas in her hand. "So you were investigating a secret message at a lighthouse island, and we were at the grocery store." She sighed. "It makes me wish I were a kid again."

"Don't feel bad, Mom. You can help us figure things out."

Upstairs in Elizabeth's room the Three-Star Detectives sat in a circle on the floor. In front of each was a drawing of the rebus. Elizabeth closed her notebook. "Okay. So we're all stuck. But here's my idea. I think we should ask Pop to help us."

"Who is this . . . Pop?" asked Peter.

"He's our grandfather," said Elizabeth. "The one who helped us with our other mysteries. He's . . . well . . ." Elizabeth wasn't sure how to describe Pop. He was old, and everything about him was slow, except for his mind. "He likes to give advice to everyone he meets, even people like the mailman or the ladies who work at the bank. And then he gets grumpy if they don't do what he says. But he's really smart. And he has good ideas." She looked at Jonathan. "So who wants to call him and tell him about the rebus?"

Jonathan turned his head and began fingering the fringe on the rug. Visiting Pop was fun, but calling him was like sweating through a 10-mile race. Most people answered the phone with a pleasant *hello*. Pop always answered with an order: *I'm eighty-two years old. Speak up and don't mumble. Enunciate!*"

"I know," said Jonathan. "Let's get Mom to call him."

A few minutes later, Jonathan sat on the top step of the spiral staircase and looked down into the living room. "She's dialing. . . Now she's talking to him. Oh-oh. Temperature's rising."

Mrs. Pollack had quickly worked herself up to a low shout. "No, Dad, I didn't say *I'm in-sane*. I said *I'm in Maine!*"

Mrs. Pollack came up the spiral staircase a few minutes later. She had a red splotch on each cheek, and her short hair was pointed in all directions. "He did have one idea. He said a rebus is usually pictures *and* letters. But this one is strange because it's only pictures. So here's what he thinks. What if Benjamin Thomas wanted to make a rebus, but he didn't want to use any letters of the alphabet? What would he do?"

Elizabeth shrugged. The other two said nothing.

"Okay, so let's say he needed the letter *m*. He didn't want to just put the letter there, so he made a picture of . . ."

"A moon!" shouted Elizabeth.

"Right. That's what Pop thought. Maybe some of the pictures are there just for their first letter. There's a picture of a moon next to a picture of an eye. So take the *m* from *moon* and put it together with eye. M—eye. You've got . . ."

"*My*," shouted Jonathan. He grabbed his paper and ran down the stairs. "I'm gonna work at the kitchen table." Elizabeth bounced onto her bed and opened her notebook.

"This is going to be easy," said Peter. "Child's play." He hurried outside and sat down underneath the oak tree in the backyard.

Elizabeth took the *d* from *diamond* and the *o* from *owl*. *Do fish m+eye heart*. *Do fish my heart*. She crossed out the words and went on to *star eye drum*. She circled the *s* from *star* and the *d* from *drum*, then put *eye* in the middle. s + eye+ d. "Side," she muttered to herself. "Then add *inn* and get *inside*." And if the picture of the waves was supposed to be the sea, then it would be *see inside*. Elizabeth felt her heart racing. Now she was getting somewhere. _____ *my heart see inside* _____. She tapped her pencil on the last three pictures. *flame till one*. Or maybe *candle till one*.

see inside . . . candle till one? see inside . . . flame till one?
What could that mean?

Elizabeth didn't want Peter the Great to beat her on this. She peered out the window. No danger yet. Peter, with his chin in his hands, sat under the tree staring at his paper.

Suddenly Jonathan shot out the door and began running around a tree. "I lit the candle! I lit the candle!" He stopped and yelled up at the window. "Hey, Elizabeth. I'm Sherlock Holmes!"

"What?" Elizabeth ran down the stairs and out the door. Jonathan circled the tree three more times, then ran back into the house.

"Your brother," whispered Peter. He tapped the middle of his forehead with his pointer finger. "He is quite all right?"

"Well, sometimes he's gets weird when he has an idea."

"Leave this to me. I go check on him." Peter disappeared into the house.

"EEEEEEH YUK!" A few minutes later Jonathan exploded out the door again. He hurled himself down on the grass, rolling around like a dog that just had a bath. Peter ran out of the house after him.

"Jonathan! What's wrong?" Mr. and Mrs. Pollack had rushed out onto the deck.

"This young chap," said Peter. "He has figured out the secret message."

"You did?" Elizabeth ran over. "So what is it?"

Jonathan stopped squirming. "It's . . . all about . . ."

He shook his head, then spit out the words like a sour grape. "It's all about LOVE!"

The Secret Message

"What do you mean . . . love?" asked Elizabeth.

"I can't say it," said Jonathan weakly. "Here, Peter, you read it." He tossed Peter a crumpled piece of paper.

Peter smoothed out the paper. "Jonathan figured out the secret message. It is this: *Jewel . . . of . . . my . . . heart . . . see . . . inside . . . little . . . one!*"

"So the picture of the burning candle means *lit*," said Elizabeth. "And the first picture means jewel, not diamond. *Jewel of my heart, see inside little one.*"

"*Jewel of my heart*," moaned Jonathan. "*Little one.*"

Elizabeth squatted down next to her brother. "Jonathan, you're so allergic to love talk you're not thinking. *See inside little one.* Don't you get it? Hattie's grandfather was telling his wife where the scroll was hidden. He probably rolled it up and put it inside a little . . . *something*."

"And when you figure out what that little *something* is, you'll know where the scroll was hidden," said Mrs. Pollack.

"So quit moaning, Jon," said Elizabeth. "You should call Hattie and Edna. Tell them you figured out the secret message."

"No, you have to call them, Elizabeth, 'cause I'm still too weak to say those love words." Jonathan stood up and kicked a ball to Peter. "But I think I could play soccer."

"Forget about soccer, Jonathan. We have to think – figure out what the *little one* means."

"It's good to move around a little," said Mr. Pollack. "Scientific research has shown that short breaks help you think more clearly."

"Right." Elizabeth called Rosewood Cottage while the others kicked the ball around. A few minutes later she came back outside. "Hattie and Edna don't know what the *little one* could be, but they're going to think about it. And if it makes you feel any better, Jon, Hattie says you're the smartest young lad in the whole United States." She gave the soccer ball a kick. "Where's Peter?"

"I don't know," said Mr. Pollack. "He went into the house while you were on the phone."

Peter suddenly appeared on the deck. He stood holding up a book in one hand, like the Statue of Liberty raising her torch. "My magnifying glass, my fingerprint powder, they do me no good with this mystery," he announced. "I must think. I will read Elizabeth's book, *How to Think Like a Detective*. And I will get *ideas*." He marched back inside.

Back in the house a few minutes later, Elizabeth knew something was strange when she found a note taped to a banana. And another one on a jar of mustard. She looked at her father. "Peter," she said.

They soon discovered scraps of paper all over the house. Each said the same thing. *See inside little one.*

Peter came out of the bathroom with a role of tape in his hand. "What ho, old chaps! I have a good idea from your book, Elizabeth."

"You got this idea from my book?"

"*How to Think Like a Detective.* Chapter 5. It says, write your most important clue and put it where you always can see it."

Peter walked around the living room, inspecting his work. He squinted at a note dangling from a potted fern. "*See inside little one.* We must think what these words are meaning. They tell us where the scroll is hidden."

"But why do you have to put the words all over the place?" asked Elizabeth.

"Because the words, they must jump out at you when you least expect. Your brain gets a big surprise and you figure out what the clue means."

"An interesting theory of brain activity," said Mr. Pollack. "The startle factor."

For the rest of the evening Elizabeth and Jonathan could go nowhere without bumping into the clue. The notes were everywhere. In the shower. On all the pillows. On every lamp. Elizabeth even found one taped to her toothbrush. *See inside little one.*

At ten o'clock Elizabeth turned off the light next to her bed. The clue whirled around in her mind, nagging and bothering like a hungry mosquito. *See inside little one*, she thought over and over again. *Little* what? Finally she rolled over and forced her eyes shut. Peter's voice suddenly trumpeted from the bottom of the stairs. "Do not forget, old chap. *See inside little one.*" Elizabeth pulled her covers over her head. She decided she liked Peter better when he was dusting for fingerprints.

The next morning Elizabeth sat up in bed, stretching as she gazed out the window. The sun was nowhere in sight. The sea and sky had melted together to a dull metal gray. Elizabeth slipped on a sweatshirt and crept down the spiral staircase. She stepped carefully, waiting for Peter to pop up and start shouting the clue. Instead, she found him on the couch, slumped down like a deflated balloon.

"What ho, old chap," he sighed. "It is not going well with me. I have thought about the clue all night and I have no ideas." Peter looked down at the floor. "I think I do not make a good detective. Fingerprints. Evidence. I like that. But . . . *das Denken* – the thinking – I do not do well. I return your detective book now." He handed Elizabeth her copy of *How to Think Like a Detective* and began taking down the notes taped to the wall.

"That doesn't mean you're a bad detective," said Elizabeth. "You just do some things better than others. Everybody's like that. You're good at technology."

"Yes," sighed Peter. "The future of crime detection." He sank back down on the couch, clicking the back of his digital camera. Elizabeth looked over his shoulder at the pictures of Turtle Island. The lighthouse. The view from the front porch. The kitchen stove. The fireplace in the dining room. "I like that little ship on the mantel," said Elizabeth. "I didn't even notice it before."

Peter straightened up slightly. "You must say that again, please."

"Say what?"

"About the ship."

"Well, I really like that little ship on the mantel."

Peter leaned over with his head in his hands and began to mutter in German. Suddenly he leaped off the sofa with a howl. Jonathan shuffled into the room yawning, with his hair sticking up on one side. "Who howled?"

"It's Peter," said Elizabeth. "He's thinking."

"By Jove, I have solved our mystery," said Peter. "You must follow my thoughts. This Benjamin Thomas chap. He calls out the name of the ship *Rebecca*. He says he hides the scroll inside the little one. You must remember the toy Hattie showed to us. The little . . . what did she call it? . . . the little sleigh made by her grandfather. This means Benjamin Thomas is working good with wood."

Elizabeth looked again at the model ship in the picture. "*See inside little one.* So you think . . . you think Hattie's grandfather carved a model ship of the *Rebecca*. And that's what he meant when he talked about the little one."

"Maybe it's hidden right there in that ship," said Jonathan. "The one on the mantel."

"No, this one is too small," said Peter. "But I know these model ships. I have seen them in Germany." He spread his hands apart. "Many are not so small. They can be over two foots . . . I mean . . . over two feets long."

Mr. and Mrs. Pollack walked in the door, back from an early morning stroll on the beach. "What's up?" asked Mrs. Pollack. "You three certainly look cheery."

"Peter figured out the clue!" shouted Jonathan. "I mean . . . I think he did."

Peter went over his idea step by step.

"Very impressive, Peter," said Mr. Pollack. "And very . . . possible. Finding a model of the ship *Rebecca*. It's certainly worth a try."

When they arrived at Rosewood Cottage for the morning meeting, Hattie opened the door before they had a chance to knock. Peter burst out with the news. Hattie said something at the same time. "We think the scroll is hidden in a model ship!"

Elizabeth gave her head a shake. Was she going crazy, or had they both said the very same thing? Hattie and Peter looked at each other. "A model ship!" Again, they spoke at the same time.

"You better come in," said Hattie. "I'm all in a muddle." Daisy led the group into the front room. Like a butler announcing their arrival, she gave two sharp barks then sat in the doorway. Peter settled into an armchair. He explained how seeing the ship on the mantel at the island gave him the idea that the scroll was hidden in a model ship.

Hattie clapped her hands. "You kids are plenty smart, I'll tell you that." She leaned back in her chair. "Course the Baker Street Girls aren't bad either. We figured out the same thing."

"Remember the letter I showed you," said Edna. "The one where Hattie's grandmother talked about the secret message. There was more in the letter, but we didn't know how important it was. Not until we heard the clue in the rug. Listen to what Hattie's grandmother wrote. It was 1893, just after Benjamin died. *It is a sad business indeed. With little means of support I must sell many of our possessions, even the beautiful little three-masted ship Benjamin had so lovingly made.*"

Hattie broke in. "It said in the history book that the *Rebecca* was a three-masted schooner. If you ask me, there's no doubt about it. My grandfather built a model of the *Rebecca.* And it would be easy as pie to hide the scroll inside the hull. The problem is, my grandmother had to sell the ship, and she didn't say who bought it."

"So what do we do?" asked Jonathan.

"It's discouraging, I know," said Edna. "It could be up in someone's attic. Or in an antique shop. Or just lost. But we figured the first place to look was the museums. I've already called the Maine Maritime Museum. And three other ones. Here's the list of phone numbers. No one has a model of the *Rebecca.* I don't know where we . . ."

"Wait a minute!" Hattie stood up. "How old was the person you talked to at the maritime museum, Edna?"

"I don't know, kind of young. But she said they didn't have the *Rebecca*. She checked in the computer."

"Computers!" snorted Hattie. "I got no use for them!"

"I say, my good lady . . . ," sputtered Peter.

"Oh, well, I guess they're handy all right. But they don't know everything." She picked up the list of phone numbers and hurried into the hallway as the others followed. On the table stood a chunky black telephone with an old-fashioned round dial. Squinting at the paper, Hattie dialed.

"Hello? Maine Maritime Museum?" Hattie had a way of barking into the phone just like their grandfather, Pop. "I'm looking for some information on a model ship. And I need to talk to someone who's been there a while. You got any old geezers workin' there?" Elizabeth looked at Peter and Jonathan. What in the world was Hattie up to? "Old geezer," she repeated loudly. "Someone who's been around for a long time. Someone over 70. The older the better." She put her hand over the receiver. "She's looking for Mr. Taylor. Says he's retired but he still spends a lot of time there."

Several minutes passed before Mr. Taylor came to the phone. After asking about the *Rebecca*, Hattie listened intently. Suddenly her face clouded over. She began writing something down.

Hattie banged down the phone. "Success," she said. "But I'm not sure you're going to like it, Edna. Years ago, some fella came to the museum. Had a model ship to sell. He said he bought it at an antique shop. The thing was a wreck. Broken masts. Most of the sails gone. The museum wasn't interested. They had enough ships and the price was high."

"And was it the *Rebecca*?" asked Edna.

"Mr. Taylor thinks so," said Hattie.

"And . . . did Mr. Taylor remember the man's name?" Elizabeth held her breath.

"He sure did. Said it was an odd name, one he'd never forget. The man's name was . . ." Hattie looked at Edna. "The man's name was Mortimer Stump."

"Mortimer Stump?" gasped Edna. She fiddled nervously with her bracelets. "Oh, my!"

"Edna, is something wrong?" asked Elizabeth.

"No, it's just . . . you see, Mortimer Stump is . . ."

"Crazy as a coot!" said Hattie. "That's what folks around here say. Course I don't hold to that. If you ask me, I'd say he's a sly old fella."

Elizabeth looked at Hattie, then at Edna. "You mean, you know him?"

"Actually, Hattie and I went to school with him," said Edna. "He lives a couple miles from here. He's an odd sort of man. Keeps to himself. Then a few years ago he decided to open a museum in his house. A kind of . . . folk art museum."

"Museum!" said Hattie. "A junkyard is more like it. Full of what people around here call *culch*. Junk."

"But do you think he still has the model ship?" asked Jonathan.

"Oh, it's possible," said Edna. "Those Stumps never throw anything away."

"This is a bit of good luck!" said Peter. "We must see this Mortimer Stump chap. We must go now!" Daisy barked and sat down by the door.

Hattie walked back into the front room and threw herself into a rocking chair. "Well, I don't know if I feel like pawin' through his culch pile."

"Hattie Pruitt. You're not still mad about that egg, are you?" Edna followed her into the room, then turned to the others. "In fifth grade Mortimer Stump put a raw egg on Hattie's chair just as she was sitting down. It made a mess of her dress."

"My *best* dress," said Hattie. "On the first day of school."

"That was a long time ago," said Edna. "And anyway, who cares if he has a mountain of junk? We have a chance to find your grandfather's model ship. And the stolen scroll."

"Well . . . maybe you're right, Edna. Sometimes I do get a little too contrary for my own good."

"Oh, wait. I just remembered something," said Elizabeth. "Mom and Dad can't drive us this morning. They're going to Spencer to meet some friends."

"Oh, that's no problem," said Hattie. "I can drive." She looked at Edna. "How about if we take the White Monster for a spin? She hasn't been out in a while."

"The White Monster?" asked Jonathan.

"That's what we call Hattie's car," laughed Edna. "It's a . . . oh, it's hard to describe. You just have to see it."

"Well? What do you think?" asked Hattie. "Should I call your parents and ask if it's all right? That way we can leave right now." All three detectives nodded. Hattie went back out into the hall.

"We better get ourselves ready for Mortimer Stump," said Edna. "I've got just the thing – a thermos full of black currant tea."

Elizabeth could smell a fruity aroma as the tea steamed from the cups. "Is this guy really crazy?"

"Like I said, he's a little odd," said Edna. "Nothing to worry about though. He's a bit rough around the edges, you might say. Course he hasn't had an easy life." Edna gazed into her cup. "You see, people here have always made their living from the sea. Catching lobster, mostly. And fishing. It's a good life, but it's hard. You could fill a book with stories just from this town. Now, Mortimer Stump was supposed to be a fisherman. Like his father and grandfather. But then . . . Oh, it's a bit of a story."

"That's okay," said Peter. "We like stories."

It all happened, Edna explained, a long time ago, when Mortimer Stump was a young man. Just before Christmas he had gone out on a boat with his father, to fish for cod. They went out a little farther than usual, and then a storm blew in. It was a howler, with the snow and wind so bad, they couldn't get back to shore. Mortimer and his father had to spend the night out at sea. They were found in the morning, half frozen, the boat dripping with icicles. Mortimer never stepped on board a boat again.

"So what did he do after that?" asked Elizabeth. She was glad to be sitting in Rosewood Cottage on a warm summer day.

"He went up north and worked in a lumber camp. That was rough work too. Years later, after his folks passed away, he came back and lived in the old house. He did odd jobs, dug for clams. Then he started his museum. I don't think many people go there."

"I feel sorry for him," said Jonathan.

"Well, Mortimer Stump is not an easy man to feel sorry for. You'll see when you meet him."

Hattie marched back into the room wearing a Boston Red Sox baseball cap and a gray cover-all that looked like a painter's suit. "Talkin' time is over. We're all set to go." She squeezed her hands into a pair of leather driving gloves. "I phoned your parents. Promised I'd stay on the back roads. Can't get into much mischief there."

"But what about money?" asked Edna. "If I know Mortimer Stump, he'll ask a pretty penny for that boat. Even if it's a wreck."

"I have a dollar," said Jonathan. He pulled a crumpled bill from his back pocket.

"And I have five Euros," said Peter. "European money."

"Don't worry about the money," said Hattie. She reached into a fat porcelain jar on the mantel and took out a handful of bills. "When my husband Sam was alive, we called this our emergency fund. Every time he'd have a good day lobsterin' he put a few dollars in here. I haven't used it in years." She counted out the bills. "One hundred and fifty dollars." She put a rubber band around the money and stuffed it into her back pocket. "That ought to do it. I'll go down the street and get the White Monster. You finish up your tea."

A few minutes later a deep rumble sounded in the distance, like the chugging of an old motorboat. Elizabeth jumped up and opened the front door. Creeping up toward the house was an enormous white car, with two fins flaring out in back like a rocket ship. Hattie's head barely peeked above the steering wheel. She rolled down the window as she pulled in front of the house. "It's not the space shuttle," she cried over the roar of the muffler. "It's a 1959 Plymouth! Climb aboard! And don't forget your coat, Edna. I wouldn't walk around in that mess wearing pink."

Edna slipped a large raincoat over her pink pants suit and locked the cottage door.

"You sit in front, Edna." Elizabeth climbed into the back, sliding across a seat as long as a couch. The sharp smell of old leather reminded her of her grandfather's car. She made room for Jonathan and Peter.

"Hold onto your hats!" yelled Hattie. She leaned forward and gripped the wheel. Slowly the car drifted away from the curb and began inching down the street. Soon a long line of cars crawled along behind them. Elizabeth craned her neck and looked at the speedometer. Hattie was cruising along at 15 miles an hour.

Just outside of town they turned onto a bumpy dirt road. The White Monster struggled through the deep ruts, bobbing and dipping like a ship on a stormy sea. At last, a lone mailbox appeared at the side of the road. Below were crooked black letters. *The Mortimer Stump Museum of American Folk Art*. In smaller letters, *Admission $2.00*.

"Two dollars!" sniffed Hattie. She turned down the long driveway. "I'll be jigged if I'll pay two dollars to get into a junkyard!"

They could see the house now, a shabby gray cottage slumped at the end of the driveway. A line of cement blocks held up a sagging porch. "I don't know," said Jonathan. "Maybe he needs the money."

"Jonathan's right," said Edna. "We shouldn't be too hard on him."

At the sound of the car, a pack of dogs raced out from behind a barn. Large. Small. Black, brown, and spotted. With a chorus of yelps, they rushed at the car. The biggest one put his front paws on Hattie's window.

Hattie opened the window a crack. "Mortimer Stump!" she yelled. "Come on out here and call off these hounds!"

A few moments later the front door opened. A tall man, as thin as a whip, stood in the doorway. He stared at the car, looking slightly amused. Taking a cigar stump out of his mouth, he snarled a command at the dogs. They slunk off behind the barn.

Edna and Hattie got out and walked up to the porch. Elizabeth and the boys stood near the car. Mortimer Stump ran his hand over the bristly gray stubble on his face. He squinted at Hattie and Edna. "Well! If it isn't the Snoopy Sisters! The ones who used to sneak around and play detective." He erupted into a high-pitched giggle.

"First of all," said Hattie. "You know we're not sisters. And we're not snoopy either. We're here on business."

Peter took a step forward. "I say, my dear chap. It would be jolly decent if you could assist us."

"Huh?" Mortimer screwed up his face, gawking at Peter as if he were a penguin who had just waddled in from Antarctica. He turned to Edna. "Is he from away?"

"He comes from Germany," said Edna crisply. "And he likes to speak *fancy* English."

"Now, don't you mind the children," said Hattie. "Like I said, we're here on business. I'm interested in buying a model ship. It's a model of the schooner *Rebecca*. I understand you may have it here."

Mortimer threw his cigar stump into the bushes. "Well now, I don't know," he said. "You'd have to look in the museum. Five admissions. Cost you ten dollars."

"We're not here to visit the . . . *museum*. We just want to buy that model ship if you have it."

"I got my rules," Mortimer drawled. "And the rules say that you don't see my collection unless you pay admission." Hattie reached into her pocket and took out a ten dollar bill. She slapped it into Mortimer's palm.

"All right, then. Come along." He led them into a large barn, dimly lit with a few bare bulbs. Down the wide center aisle was a line of tables littered with baskets, old bottles, and broken toys. Behind the tables rose a mountain of . . . Now Elizabeth knew what Hattie meant by *culch*. Butter churns, lobster traps, chairs, boat oars, and bedposts were mixed with rubber boots and tangled-up fish nets. Elizabeth stared in dismay. If Benjamin Thomas's model ship was in there, they would need a bulldozer to get it out.

"You call this art?" muttered Hattie.

"I sure do," cackled Mortimer. "Gen-u-ine folk art." He took a fresh cigar out of his pocket and stuck it in his mouth without lighting it. "Let's see now. You say you were wantin' a model ship." Mortimer strolled down the aisle, straightening out things on the tables as he passed. He stopped at the last table and leaned over to look underneath. "Right here is where I keep it. Under this blanket for safekeeping."

Elizabeth leaned forward as he lifted the edge of a moth-eaten red blanket. She stared at what was underneath, unable to believe her eyes. It was a bird cage.

Mortimer straightened up. "Now, where did that ship get to? I was awful sure it was here." He shook his head slowly. "I know I didn't sell it. Or did I?"

Elizabeth closed her eyes. They were so close to solving their mystery. The ship had to be here somewhere.

"Time to hit the dirt." Jonathan dove under the table and disappeared behind a stack of old magazines. On his hands and knees, he poked around in the piles of junk underneath the table. Elizabeth followed him with her eyes. There. Behind an old lobster trap was the tip of a mast. With a scrap of sail hanging from it!

"That's right, sonny!" called Mortimer. "You just push it out here." With a scraping sound, the two-foot long hull of a model ship appeared, followed by a very dusty Jonathan. Mortimer Stump bent down. "Yup, she's a beauty, all right." He took the bulky ship in his arms and held it out. It was a sorry-looking mess, with three broken masts, the sails in shreds and ropes in a hopeless tangle. But none of that mattered. The bottom of the ship was in good shape. And just the right size for hiding a small scroll.

Edna rushed forward and rubbed the dirt off a small metal plate on the deck. "*Rebecca*! It says *Rebecca*!"

"*Wunderbar*![7]" said Peter. "This is a bit of all right."

Mortimer smiled. "You said it, sonny. This sure is a fine piece of art." He blew a cloud of dust off the deck as he set the heavy ship on the floor. "If you ladies want to buy it, I'll give you a special deal. Since we went to school together." He chewed his cigar for a moment. "Two hundred dollars. Take it or leave it. No bargaining."

Hattie took the wad of bills out of her pocket. "I've got one hundred and forty dollars. Not a penny more."

Mortimer Stump plucked the money out of her hand. "On second thought, that'll be just fine."

---

[7] *Wunderba*r (VUHN der bar). Wonderful.

Hattie grabbed the ship and headed toward the door. "Next stop – Rosewood Cottage!"

Elizabeth scrambled into the car and sat in back between Peter and Jonathan. The three of them held onto the ship as they bumped their way back to Stone Harbor.

Hattie turned onto Main Street and dropped them off in front of Rosewood Cottage. She leaned over and called out the window. "Just don't look inside the ship until I get back."

Elizabeth glanced over at the library, relieved to see no sign of Mrs. Patterson. She and Peter carried the model ship into the house, with Daisy racing around them in joyful circles. "Just set it right here on the table," said Edna. "And you go sit in your corner, Daisy."

"I can't wait for Hattie to come so we can open it up," said Edna. She walked toward the window. "She should be . . . What? I don't believe it. This can't be!" The fear in Edna's words made Elizabeth spin around. "What's wrong?"

Edna stood by the window with one hand cupped over her mouth. Slowly she lowered her hand and pointed to the small table by the window. "That!"

Two objects lay side by side on the table. A copy of *The History of Stone Harbor* and a sheet of paper with faded brown ink. At the top were the words *Portland Hospital, September 21, 1890.* Elizabeth knew immediately what she was seeing. It was the letter with the strange confession of the mystery man – the man they now knew to be Hattie's grandfather. And the history book about Stone Harbor. Both had been stolen from Rosewood Cottage days ago.

"How can this be?" muttered Edna. "They're back. Exactly where they were before they disappeared!"

The Truth Comes Out

"I'm burnin' to see what's inside that ship!" Hattie rushed into the front room, pulling off her driving gloves. "Let's get to it! We should . . . why are you all standing by the window?"

"Strange happenings," said Peter solemnly.

Edna motioned for Hattie to come over. "You won't believe this. The letter and the book that were stolen. They're right here, back on the table. But the front door was locked. How in the world did they get here?"

"There's something sticking out of the book," said Jonathan. "A piece of paper."

Hattie squinted down at the book as if it were a coiled-up snake ready to strike. Carefully she plucked the slip of paper from between the pages. "What on earth!" She held it out to the others. Scrawled across the paper were the words *Call me*. It was signed *Tom*. Hattie's nephew!

Without a word Hattie disappeared into the hallway and returned a few moments later. "I just called Tom. He's coming right over." She paced across the room a few times then planted herself in a high-backed armchair. "I hope you don't mind, but I don't want to look inside the ship just yet. I can't set my mind on anything until I find out what's going on with Tom."

Elizabeth looked longingly at the model ship. She couldn't wait to find out if the Chinese scroll was hidden inside. But she was as uneasy as Hattie. What did Tom have to do with the stolen letter and book?

Ten minutes later Tom strode into the room, his face tight and serious. The Three-Star detectives sat on the couch, with Hattie and Edna across from them in the winged armchairs. Without saying a word, Tom placed a chair in front of the fireplace and sat down facing the others. Daisy gave a few hopeful wags of her tail, then settled down next to Tom and put her head on her paws.

"There's something that all of you need to know," said Tom. He put his hands on his knees, small hands, Elizabeth noticed, just like Hattie's. "So here goes. I was the one who took the letter and the history book. And the two books from the Spencer Library." Tom looked at the floor. "When we brought you home after dinner last week, Edna left her sweater in the car. I didn't notice until Lenny and I drove away. When I came back, the door was unlocked, so I just let myself in. I put the sweater on a chair in the front room. That's when I saw the book and the letter . . . and took them."

Jonathan and Peter were leaning so far forward they almost fell off the couch.

"But why?" asked Hattie.

"Because I was hoping you and Edna would give up the case. But now . . . I can't keep it secret any longer. Aunt Hattie, I know who the mystery man was. The man with the fever who confessed to stealing the scroll. He was . . ."

Hattie reached over and patted her nephew's hand. "I know, dear. The thief was Benjamin Thomas, my grandfather. And your great grandfather."

"You mean . . . you already know?"

"Oh, the children figured it out days ago, Tom. While you were out of town. It's a long story. And we'll tell you about it later. But how did *you* know Benjamin Thomas was the mystery man?"

Tom leaned back and loosened his grip on his knees. "It all started a few months ago when I decided to do a family history project. It was going to be a surprise. You see, I was curious about Benjamin Thomas. No one in the family seemed to know much about him. I looked at all kinds of things – newspaper articles, old crew lists and captains' diaries. You'd be amazed at how much I was able to find out about him."

"So when we told you that the mystery man talked about Stone Harbor and called out for Rebecca," said Edna, "you knew right away who he was."

"That's right. I knew that Benjamin was the only one who had survived the sinking of the *Rebecca*. And I even knew he had been in the hospital in Portland in 1890." He turned to Hattie. "Family is important to you, Aunt Hattie. I knew you'd be upset if you found out about your grandfather. That's why I didn't want you to know. Why stir up this old mystery? Get everyone in town talking and gossiping about Grandfather Benjamin? The theft has almost been forgotten. I thought we should just leave it that way." He gave a half smile. "Of course, I didn't know you'd hook up with an international detective agency."

Peter straightened up and smiled. Elizabeth felt relieved. Everything was falling into place, except . . .

"We were at the old inn a few days ago," she said. "Someone tried to scare us. It wasn't . . . I mean, you wouldn't have . . ."

"I don't understand," said Tom. "Something happened at the Jeremiah Coffin Inn?"

Hattie described their late-night trip to the inn and the strange intruder who frightened them.

"I have no idea who that could have been, Aunt Hattie. But I don't like the idea of someone trying to scare you. Why in the world would anyone do that?"

Elizabeth's forehead tightened. Who had followed them into the inn that night?

Tom leaned forward. "Anyway, I'm sorry about all this foolishness, Aunt Hattie. I hope you're not mad. And you either, Edna."

Edna smiled and shook her head.

"We're not mad," said Hattie. "We know you meant well. But one thing confounds me. Why did my grandfather steal the scroll?"

"I can't say exactly," said Tom, "but I do know that Benjamin didn't like the town of Stone Harbor. You already know he was the only survivor when the *Rebecca* sank. But there's more. One year earlier he had been on another ship that sank. It was just a coincidence, of course. But sailors are superstitious. Benjamin became known as a Jonah. That meant someone who was cursed and brought bad luck to a ship. None of the local captains would hire him."

"So that's why Benjamin Thomas had to leave Stone Harbor," said Hattie. "He left his family behind and sailed out from Portland. He must have taken the scroll sometime before he left town."

Tom raised his hands. "I should have told the truth about Benjamin Thomas right away. Even though it would hurt you. Of course either way, we're not going to find the Chinese scroll."

The words *Chinese scroll* struck like lightning. Five heads turned in the direction of the round table. Hattie grinned. "Don't be so sure of that, Tom. By the way, did you happen to notice anything different when you came in?"

"Just that old model ship on the table. I hate to say it, Aunt Hattie, but it's a real mess. I hope you didn't pay too much."

"Oh, we had to shell out a bit of money all right. We found the ship at that junkyard Mortimer Stump calls a museum. Now I know it sounds crazy, Tom, but we think . . . we *hope* that the stolen Chinese scroll is hidden in that ship." Hattie walked over to the round table and waved for the others to follow. "And now, my friends, it's time."

Elizabeth rose from the couch, squeezing her hands into fists to keep them from trembling.

Inside the Little One

Silently, the group settled into chairs at the round table. Elizabeth looked at the ship, with its broken masts and shredded sails. Their trail of clues was at an end. If they were right, the tattered ship hid a treasure missing for over one hundred years. If they were wrong, their case was over. They would never find the scroll.

Hattie jumped up and turned on a lamp. The sky had darkened and the first drops of rain spattered against the window. "No use puttin' it off," she said. "This is it. All or nothing."

Peter leaned over and poked through the tangle of string on the deck. Toward the back he discovered a small hatch. Carefully, he pried it open with his finger. A square opening led to the dark belly of the ship.

"My hands are little," said Jonathan. "Let me try." He squeezed his hand into the opening and groped around. "I don't think . . . Wait. I feel something hard, like wood. But it's too big to pull out."

"There must be some way to get inside," said Edna. "We don't want to tear it apart."

"I know where to start," said Hattie. She hurried out of the room and came back with a rag in her hand. "There must be a hundred years of dust on this thing."

As she carefully wiped the back of the ship, the rusty head of a small screw could be seen. Soon they were able to remove a panel at the back of the ship.

"And now – the moment of truth." Hattie reached in and pulled out a long narrow wooden box. She undid a tiny hook and tipped the box. Slowly an object slid out. A long . . . cream colored . . . rolled-up . . . scroll!

"Well, I'll be hornswoggled!" shouted Hattie. "The Chinese scroll!" She hugged Tom, who was moving his lips without any words coming out.

Jonathan exploded out of his chair, waving his arms from side to side over his head. "Oh, yeah. I'm feelin' good today!" Daisy joined him, then Peter, then Elizabeth. They circled the room in a wild victory dance as Edna tapped the beat with her cane. Peter suddenly stopped in front of the window. Mr. Edmond was on the sidewalk in front of the house. He hurried away at the sound of Peter's *What ho, my good man*!

"Attention, detectives," called Hattie. "The Baker Street Girls have got a little surprise. We can't unroll the scroll yet. Someone needs to be here." She disappeared into the hallway. Elizabeth could hear her dial the phone. "We're ready for you now," she said in a low voice. "Can you come?"

They moved the ship aside and set the rolled-up scroll in the middle of the table. Daisy was shut up in a back room, where she protested with an occasional bark. At the sound of a knock on the door, Hattie hurried into the hallway. She returned with a young woman whose smooth black hair was pulled into a long pony tail.

"This is Li Ming," announced Hattie. "From Shanghai, China. She's the lady professor I told you about. The one who gave us the art book."

Li Ming nodded and smiled as she was introduced to Tom and the detectives. She moved over to the table. "So this is the stolen scroll you told me about, Hattie."

"That's right. Stolen from the Stone Harbor Town Hall in 1890. And the history book says it was made during the Sung Dynasty. We didn't want to unroll it until you were here."

121

"If that history book is right," said Li Ming, "we're about to see a silk scroll painted in China nearly a thousand years ago."

Hattie leaned over and gently began to smooth out the scroll. The first thing Elizabeth saw was writing in the top corner. Delicate Chinese characters stood out on the cream-colored silk, each one like a tiny picture. Underneath was a painting – a single branch of a fruit tree blooming against a garden wall. Elizabeth stared at the tiny white flowers. How could brush strokes on a piece of silk make flowers so fresh she could almost smell spring in the air? A spring day from a thousand years ago and halfway across the world.

Everyone looked at Li Ming, waiting for her to say something. She stared at the scroll for a long time. Finally she spoke quietly, as if she were in a church. "You have honored me by asking me here today. This treasure . . . is exquisite. And I do believe it is from the Sung Dynasty. The scroll shows what we call *the three perfections*. Painting. Calligraphy, which is the art of making beautiful Chinese writing. And poetry."

Elizabeth leaned over to take a closer look at the writing. "You mean the Chinese writing is a poem?"

"Yes. The poem describes the plum blossoms in the painting. You see, in China, these blossoms make people think of hope and courage. Plum trees bloom very early in the spring. Such delicate flowers, and yet so strong they bloom even in the snow."

"And what does it say?" asked Tom.

"The poem is very simple. Like the painting. The idea is to make much out of just a little. So a few words or a painting of just one branch brings a whole spring day to life." Li Ming held her finger just above the Chinese characters. "This is how I would say it in English: *Soft white petals wave at the sky. Laughing, they dance with the wind.*"

"That's lovely," said Edna.

Li Ming straightened up. "Hattie told me that you know about the imperial scrolls. I don't want to get your hopes up, but it's possible that this poem was written by an emperor or an empress."

An empress. One thousand years ago. Elizabeth couldn't take her eyes off the scroll.

"Of course we need to show it to someone with more knowledge than I have. We could . . ."

The bang of a door announced Daisy's escape. She charged into the room with her whiskers flying, took one look at Li Ming, and jumped into her lap. "Ah, my friend Daisy. I see you have escaped."

"It's one of her best skills," laughed Edna.

"Well, as long as Daisy has interrupted us," said Hattie, "I have a question. How do we give this scroll back to the town? If you ask me, I think we should do it with a little hoopla."

"Oh, yes," said Peter, "I would very much like this – how do you say the word – this *hoopla*."

"But we can't get a whole town together," said Edna.

Hattie shot up from her chair. "Why not? The town clerk could call a town meetin'. And we could put up signs inviting all the tourists too. Tell 'em to come hear a surprise announcement. People are awful curious. They'll come like cats chasing a string. And that way all the suspects will be gathered up in one place."

"Suspects?" asked Peter. "But the mystery. We have solved it."

"Not entirely," said Hattie. "I won't rest easy until I know who was clompin' around in the Jeremiah Coffin Inn."

Two days later, Stone Harbor had an evening meeting no one would ever forget. Tourists and townspeople streamed into the town hall. Elizabeth recognized a few people – Li Ming, Mr. and Mrs. Edmond, and the librarian Mrs. Patterson. Tom came in with his son Lenny and

Lenny's girlfriend. Even Mortimer Stump made an appearance. Elizabeth and the boys sat with Mr. and Mrs. Pollack in the front row.

The audience turned as Hattie and Edna made their entrance. Edna made her way slowly with her cane, floating down the center aisle in a flowered dress. Hattie, walking stiffly in her lavender dress, carried a large wooden box. They sat down next to Elizabeth.

"Li Ming took us to a museum in Boston," she whispered. "With an expert in Chinese art. It's an imperial scroll, all right. With a poem by an empress of China. Very rare."

With a bang of the gavel, the town clerk opened the meeting. "Ladies and gentlemen," she began. "We have called this unusual meeting tonight at the request of Mrs. Hattie Pruitt and Mrs. Edna Mancini. They have something to announce." The clerk cast a doubtful look at Hattie. "Supposedly something of great importance to the town of Stone Harbor."

Hattie stood up, arm in arm with Edna. Mr. Pollack helped them onto the stage. "I'm not one for long speeches," began Hattie. "So I'll get right to the point. Back in 1890 a valuable Chinese scroll was stolen from the town of Stone Harbor. Taken from a display case right in this very building. Now, over the years there's been talk about Edna's grandmother bein' the thief. I always knew that was a lot o' hogwash. And tonight we're going to prove it. Tonight we're here to tell you the real thief has been discovered." Hattie paused as whispers rippled through the room. "I'm sorry to tell you, but the thief is . . . The thief is my own grandfather, Benjamin Thomas."

The whispers turned into a roar. Hattie spoke over the noise. "Now, we are lucky to have some well-known detectives summerin' here this year." She motioned for Elizabeth and the boys to stand up with her. "These youngsters have been workin' with me and Edna. And together we have solved the case. The Chinese scroll missing for over one hundred years has been found! All these years it's been hidden in a model ship made by my grandfather." Hattie opened the wooden box and unrolled the scroll. Mortimer Stump's cigar slipped out of his mouth and fell on the floor.

The clerk gave up trying to keep any order. The audience was on its feet, crowding around the scroll, asking questions. Peter mingled with the crowd, handing out his business cards.

"Take it easy, now. Everyone in your seat," shouted the clerk. "If you have questions, raise your hand. I'm sure we'd all like to know how this mystery was solved." For the rest of the meeting the detectives answered questions, describing the trail of clues that led to the scroll. After Hattie and Edna handed the scroll to the town treasurer, Mrs. Pollack went on stage to give them a bouquet of flowers. A few people got up and moved toward the door.

"Not so fast!" Hattie waved her hand toward the people near the door. "You just come in here and sit down. There's one more item of business." She grabbed the gavel and gave it a bang. "A few days ago our investigation took us to the Jeremiah Coffin Inn. Late at night. Someone followed us in there and about scared us to death." Hattie stared out into the audience. "Now, this is a small town. And someone in this room knows who did it. I'm not tryin' to get anyone in trouble. I just want to know who it was. Us detectives don't like loose ends."

"I suspect that Mr. Edmond chap," whispered Peter. Elizabeth looked over at Mr. Edmond. He was the picture of innocence, looking over his shoulder to see if anyone would come forward.

Hattie waited for a minute, then gave a final bang with the gavel. "I declare the meetin' over. But I'll stay around for awhile, in case anyone wants to tell me something."

Edna made her way off the stage and sank into her chair. She fanned her bright pink face. "We haven't had so much excitement in years."

A photographer from the local newspaper took a group photo. The Three-Star Detectives stood next to the Baker Street Girls. Mortimer Stump slipped in at the last minute and stood grinning next to Hattie. "You're all invited to my museum," he called out to the audience. "Featurin' a special display on the Mystery of the Chinese Scroll. Come see the spot where the mystery was solved."

A few minutes later, Peter gave Elizabeth a nudge. "Where's Hattie? I am not seeing her." Elizabeth glanced around the room. Hattie was nowhere in sight. Tom and his son Lenny seemed to be looking for her also.

Suddenly, Hattie appeared from a side door. "Bingo! The last piece of the puzzle just fell into place." She stood next to Edna and pulled the other detectives into a huddle. "Here's the scoop," Hattie whispered. "The person who scared the wits out of us was . . . You'll never guess. Lenny's girlfriend."

"Lenny's girlfriend? But why?" asked Elizabeth. "We don't even know her. Why would she want to scare us?"

"Because she thought she was scaring someone else. You see, Tom was out of town that night. He didn't know it, but Lenny and his friends planned to spend the night at the inn. Show how brave they were. Course Lenny called it off when he found out we would be there. But his girlfriend didn't know. She decided to give the boys a good scare. Make 'em think old Mad Dan the pirate was stompin' around. When she saw Edna and me, she realized her mistake. She was so embarrassed, she never told anybody until just now."

By this time the town hall had almost emptied out. Mr. and Mrs. Pollack stood talking to Li Ming and Mrs. Patterson. Mr. and Mrs. Edmond waved at the detectives from across the room. "I would like to offer my congratulations," called Mr. Edmond. Peter started walking over to him, but Mr. Edmond held up his still-purple hand. "I think it's wiser to admire you from afar." He took his wife's arm and hurried out the door.

"Poor Mr. Edmond," cackled Hattie. "I never did see a man who has more trouble with dogs and children. But, anyway, let's all get along to Rosewood Cottage. We've got some celebratin' to do."

As the group headed down the street, Elizabeth stopped for a moment and glanced back at the narrow old town hall. Light streamed from the large windows and poured out the open doors. Then, suddenly, the windows went dark as the lights were turned off for the night. The wide doors clicked shut. Elizabeth felt as if a book had been closed. The dark, empty building told her their mystery was over. Soon Peter would go home to Germany, and she and Jonathan would go back to Indiana. Life would return to normal.

When the doorbell rang on a drizzly Saturday in November, Elizabeth waited for someone else to go to the door. She had been puzzling over her social studies project for half an hour. Why did she ever volunteer to build a mini windmill out of Popsicle sticks? Her talking parakeet Fritzi pattered around on her desk, pushing the sticks onto the floor. "Dirty," he chattered. "Take a bath."

"Special delivery for the Three-Star Detective Agency." Mr. Pollack's voice sounded up the stairs. Elizabeth and Jonathan nearly collided as they burst out of their rooms. Their parents stood in the living room, with a package neatly wrapped in brown paper. The return address read *Town of Stone Harbor*.

Elizabeth pulled out two brightly-wrapped presents and a short note. *Because of your help, the Chinese scroll is once again on display in the Town Hall. The residents of Stone Harbor, Maine, send you these gifts in appreciation of your fine detective work. The same gift has been sent to Peter Hoffmann in Hamburg, Germany.*

"And there's a note from Hattie," continued Elizabeth, quickly skimming the words. "She said she's having the model ship fixed up. And Tom is going to help her find out what happened to the mystery rug. And listen to this, Jonathan. *Edna and I must be going soft in our old age. We gave Mortimer Stump the old letter, the one with the words of my grandfather's confession. Mortimer wanted it for his display. The old coot is happy as a clam. His museum is now called The Mortimer Stump Museum of Local History.*"

"I say," said Jonathan. "That's a bit of all right!" He picked up one of the gifts. "And now we can open our presents." He opened the box and peered in. "It looks like . . . a bottle!" Elizabeth looked into her box. "I have the same thing." She pulled out a small bottle, sitting on its side and set into a wooden base.

"I can't believe it! It's so beautiful!" Elizabeth held the bottle up. Inside was a tiny ship carved out of wood – ship with sails billowing proudly from three tall masts. A perfect model of the *Rebecca*.

Later in the afternoon Elizabeth stood alone in her room. Carefully she placed the ship on the top shelf of a small wooden bookcase. It was her mystery shelf, with a memento from each of their cases. Elizabeth gazed at the objects on the shelf – bits of glass worn smooth by the sea, a postcard showing the lobby of an elegant hotel, a picture of herself and Jonathan in front of a castle door. And now, the ship *Rebecca*. She slid the ship a few inches to the side. She wanted to leave plenty of room for another mystery. Just in case.

She took her red spiral detective notebook off the bottom shelf. Peter's business card slipped out as she opened the front cover. *Peter Hoffmann, Super Sleuth Extraordinaire. Three-Star Detective Agency.* Elizabeth picked up the card. Sherlock Holmes had his Doctor Watson. She had Peter the Great and . . .

"Hey, Elizabeth! Mom says I can get a hissing cockroach for my birthday. If you want, I'll let it sit on your finger."

Elizabeth sighed. For better or for worse . . . she had Jonathan.